The Cabin

LaRhonda N. Felton

LaRhonda N. Felton

Email: **LaRhondaNFelton@gmail.com**

Facebook.com/AuthorLaRhondaNFelton

Instagram: @Author_LaRhondaNFelton

Edited, Formatted, and Published via *iWrite4orU*: **www.iWrite4orU.com**

Cover Image Obtained from iStockPhoto.com

Designed by The Logo Queen Jax

ISBN: 978-0-9998842-8-7

Library of Congress Control Number: 2020925501

Printed in the United States of America

Dedication

The Cabin, my third publication, is dedicated to LOVE. I know that God is love and through Him, we're blessed with the warmth it brings.

Love, in my opinion, is the one emotion that supersedes all others. It's the driving force for life and no matter how you feel about love at the moment, it's what we all need and desire at the core of our beings.

2020 has demonstrated that love is a precious commodity that we all benefit from and can use a little more of. Not that I needed a year to explain love to me, because I've always known what real love is capable of. If you have loved and lost, as some of us have, don't shy away. Love on you until you feel that you can take the chance on letting someone else in.

A new love evokes the butterflies in your stomach of your first teen crush and the euphoria of all that makes you smile. An older love can be resolute and comforting while still triggering those new love vibes.

Love sincerely and be open to expand your capacity to love deeper than you ever have before.

xoxo

~The Poetic Gemini

LaRhonda N. Felton

CHAPTER 1

Jaliyah

My reality comes undone as I nearly pass out in the sun.

I couldn't shake the feeling
And work wasn't sinking in
I decided to end my misery
And visit with my friend
I got in the car
And of course, I needed gas
He's always driving my car
Making me want to kill his ass
The reason he got a motorcycle
But every day it rained
He was in my car
Ignoring my complaints
I worked from home
So, I was inside all day
But when I wanted to leave
I needed to stop for gas along the way

I grabbed lunch
And pumped my gas
While men at the gas station
Cat called as I passed
Something was off
I felt it in my bones
I was anxious and sad
And didn't want to be alone
She would help with my confusion
Make some sense of this bad mood
We would laugh, sip on wine
And eat some good food

I parked in the driveway
And rang the doorbell
Does she have company?
That sounded like a yell

The Cabin

Maybe I should've called first
Oops, they were getting it in
Hell, I wouldn't disturb her
I thought to myself, finish him friend

And suddenly I heard
An all too familiar sound
When his voice commanded
"Turn that ass around."

The rush of heat
Made me feel faint
I thought to myself
I know the fuck they ain't

I felt a hand on my back
"Come with me
You need some water
And to get out of this heat."
I was too weak to protest
I had to be wrong
Had this been my suspicion
Nagging me all along

The neighbor sat me down
In his backyard on a chaise
The Ducati Panigale
Was staring me in the face

He instructed, "Take a few deep breaths
In through your nose, out through your mouth
I was hoping you didn't pass out
On the porch at her house
This has been going on
Since last year
I thought he was her man
As much as he's over here."

LaRhonda N. Felton

He opened my water
I guess I looked too weak
"Sip it slow," he advised
I couldn't even speak
He kept on talking
I must've zoned out
I had no idea what the hell
He was talking about
He shook me and asked
"Hey are you listening?
Do you need a wet cloth?
I can get one for you
To help you cool off
I'm sorry this happened
That you found out this way
I knew it was coming
Didn't know it would be today."

I finally found the words
That were scrambled in my brain

"Can you please bring that cloth?
I feel faint again."

"I'll be right back
Just stay in your seat
I'm a doctor on vacation
Not looking for a patient to treat."

I wanted to scream
And the water made me sick
I couldn't believe my eyes
And the reality of this shit
This talking ass neighbor
He knew a hell of a lot
And he could see her entire house
From this backyard spot

He brought me the cloth
I saw the stethoscope around his neck
"There's no need for that
I haven't passed out yet."

"I wasn't sure
Shock can be hell
And with the way you were looking
I couldn't really tell
So, are you his girlfriend?
Or his ex?
As much as he's here
Y'all can't be having much sex."

And he was right
He barely touched me
That motorcycle purchase
Kept us arguing
But it was more than that
Things had been off for a while
And I may have to decide very soon
If I'm going to keep our child

The neighbor probed, "Are you okay now?
What are you going to do?
You need to decide something
He will be coming out soon."

"How do you know so much?
And how long have you been watching?"
"My cameras are rolling 24/7
And I don't plan on stopping."

I got up to leave
"Thanks for your help."
I didn't know what to do
I trusted her like no one else

LaRhonda N. Felton

He offered, "Come back by
If you ever want to see
I kept the recordings
Stored in my system's memory."

I left Charae's house
With the intention of going home
My mind was racing and distracted
I needed some time alone
I had been driving for a while
Appetite long gone
Jayson had called three times
I just didn't want to go home
I had crossed the state line
More than a hundred miles ago
Heading to my family's cabin
At least it was somewhere close

It was getting late
And the cabin may not have power
Renovations aren't complete
I may have to take a cold shower
That was the last thing I needed
But I couldn't turn back
I needed to sort some things out
At home, I couldn't do that
I turned on the road to the cabin
I could see lights in the distance
And a truck parked in front
Who in the hell is this?

I dialed my parents
Hopefully, they were still up
I needed them to tell me
Who was the driver of this truck

The smell of the magnolia trees
Caused flashes from my childhood

The Cabin

My dad picked up asking
"What you know good?"
I smiled, "Hi Daddy"
"Hey, Baby Girl, are you okay?
I'm glad you called me
But even for you, it's really late."

"I'm okay, Daddy
Just came to the cabin
There are lights on and a truck parked
I wanted to know what's happening?"

"Oh, that's just the contractor
He's living there until the work is complete
I didn't know you were going there
He's going to be there a few more weeks."

"Oh, I didn't know
I guess I'll head home."

"Baby girl it's so late
Are you driving alone?"

"Yes, Daddy
But I'll be okay."

"No, I will call him now
You go on in and stay.
He's the only son
Of my old army friend
He will welcome the company
And I know you will love him.
As a friend of course
I know you have a boyfriend
And even though I don't like him
That's not worth rehashing."

"Daddy, are you sure?
I don't want to be any trouble."

LaRhonda N. Felton

"Baby Girl, go on up there
I'm calling him on the double."

"Thanks, Daddy
I will leave at first light
I'm tired of driving
Ready to rest tonight."

"Where are you headed, Baby Girl?
You're traveling rather late
Don't kid your old man
Are you sure everything is okay?"

"I'm sure, Daddy
I'm just fine
I came out for a drive
And lost track of time
I then realized
I was closer to the cabin than I was to home
And I came here
Thinking I'd be alone."

"Okay let me call him
He can help you get settled
I'm sure with everything in disarray
He knows the way around much better."

After dad hung up
I debated driving away
But I was too tired
And decided to stay
The front door opened
And I couldn't believe my eyes
This man was gorgeous
And shit, he was fine
This isn't a good idea
I should probably leave
But I couldn't pull off
He was coming toward me

The Cabin

"Hi, I'm Sebastian
Come on inside."
He had an amazing accent
That he could hardly hide

"I don't want to impose
I didn't know anyone was here."
I could hear my dad on his phone
Saying, "Go on inside my dear."

He was at least 6'3
Caramel complexion with hazel-green eyes
Bowlegged and sexy
With a gorgeous smile

"Do you need help with your bags?"

"No, I hadn't planned to stay
I came out for a drive
And ended up out this way."

He was saying good night to my dad
While opening my car door
He smiled, "Yes Sir, I will
She's in good hands, rest assured."

"I'm sorry for just popping up
You don't have to cater to me."

"It's so quiet out here
I'm glad for the company."

I got my purse
And headed inside
I was astounded
My face didn't hide my surprise

"Oh my gosh, it looks amazing!
My dad will be pleased."

"Thanks, I hope you find everything
Suitable to your needs."

"I'm sure I will
Your work is impeccable
And what is my nose picking up
That smells so delectable?"

"Oh, that's just a little dinner
I know it's late
But I worked longer than usual today
Would you like a plate?"

"No, no I will shower
And go on to sleep
I won't disrupt your evening
I promise I won't make a peep."

"Come on now, you're here
We can share a meal
I hate eating alone
You're doing me a favor, for real."

"Okay, I will join you for dinner
Thanks for being so kind
But let me shower first."

"Absolutely, take your time."

I didn't go into the master suite
Figuring that's where he slept
I picked the next largest suite
Which was down the hall on the left

I powered my phone off
And sat in the chair
Tired from the day's events
It all felt so unfair
My mind was racing

The Cabin

And I was tired
I needed to ask Sebastian
If he had logs for a fire
Each suite was like a mini cottage
Some large and some small
And it's always cooler at night
Especially with it being Fall
The bathroom was spectacular
He'd really outdone himself
I couldn't wait to see the kitchen
Along with everything else
The shower felt wonderful
With the rainfall shower-head
If I wasn't starving
I would go straight to bed
Returning to the room
The fireplace had been lit
It was so warm and peaceful
I didn't realize how much I needed it

I heard a knock at the door
"Is everything okay?"
"Yes, thanks for the fire
I'm on my way."

On the foot of the bed
I noticed some clothes
I didn't bring any of mine
I'd planned to dine in the robe
Sebastian left some socks
And what appeared to be his T-shirt
I put it on
And it fit long like a skirt
It smelled amazing
Could it be his cologne?
I needed to get out of here
And take my ass home

Just then my stomach growled
Reminding me of my predicament
Possibly pregnant by a cheater
How the hell could I forget
I needed to be sure
I made a mental note to call my G-Y-N
I headed to the dining room
As my stomach growled again

Sebastian stood, "There you are
I hope you didn't mind
Me starting that fire
And lending you that shirt of mine."

"I appreciate it
Thank you so much
I don't want to be a bother
Sharing your dinner is more than enough."

"Well, I hope you enjoy
It's seared white bass with lemon and thyme
Mixed vegetables with rice pilaf
And a dessert that's a favorite of mine."
"What dessert is that?
If I may inquire."

"Certainly, you may
But first let me stoke the fire."

Everything looked delicious
I was ready for my plate

"And the piece de resistance
Is my chocolate mousse cake."

"Oh my God
That looks divine."

"Let's dig in."

He was reading my mind.

The first bite of white bass
I nearly passed out
It was like the awakening
Of every taste bud in my mouth
Who is this man?
He didn't cook this alone
I ate an entire section
And didn't find one bone

"You're awfully quiet
How does the food taste?"
The answer to his question
Was evident by my empty plate

"It was amazing
Are you sure you aren't a chef?"

"You learn to do a lot of things
When forced to take care of yourself
You ready for dessert?"

"Yes, but just a little piece."

"Okay, a sliver then
But let me know what you think."

The first bite
Smooth, velvety and rich

I didn't mean to
Vocalize my thoughts
When I murmured, "Oh shit."

He asked, "Is that a good thing?"

I couldn't even speak
I savored a little longer
"Please forgive me
That didn't come out right
It did, but not quite
Everything has been exquisite
I will sleep well tonight."

He smiled, "I'm glad you enjoyed it
I'm going to get this cleaned up."

"No, let me do that
You've already done too much."

"I would have to clean it
If I were here alone."

"But you're not
So, get out of here. Now, go on."

I cleaned the kitchen
It gave me time to think
About how long my relationship
Has truly been out of sync
I put the leftovers away
And turned off the lights
Sebastian was in the dining room

He questioned, "Are you turning in for the night?"

"I am, I'm tired
It's been a long day
And the last thing you need
Is for me to be in your way."

"If you're tired
Going to bed, I understand
But this is like, your home
I'm just the hired handyman."

The Cabin

"With what you've done here
Handyman doesn't come close
You're more like an architect
And a chef that doesn't boast."

"Thank you for the compliment
Are you sure you're okay?
I listen well without judgment
If there's something you need to say."

"I'm good, thanks for offering."

"I hear you, but your energy says different
Just know that I don't mind
If you need me to listen."

"Thank you, Sebastian,
You are far too kind
But you have a life of your own
No need boring you with mine."

"Listen, Jaliyah, I know women
And something is wrong
You drove to what you thought
Was an empty cabin, in the dark, all alone."

I wasn't ready to talk about it
He was nice, but a stranger nonetheless
"I'm going in for the night
I think that's probably what's best."

"I didn't mean to pry
It was just a mere observation
I never meant to intrude
Forgive me for my invasion."

"No harm done
Thank you for everything."

"You're welcome, sleep well
Let me know if you need anything."

I went back to my suite
And turned on my phone
I had several more messages
I wished he'd leave me alone

I fell asleep almost immediately
And was awakened by hard rain
I sat on the side of the bed
My phone was ringing again
I answered it confirming
"Yes, Jayson, I am fine."

He asked, "Where the hell have you been
All this time?"

"It doesn't matter
Once again, I'm okay."

"What was I supposed to think?
You've been gone all damn day."

"Were you really that concerned?
I find that hard to believe
But it's very late
And you're disturbing my sleep."

"Why in the hell are you trippin'?
Complaining about sleep
I've been calling you all day
You haven't been answering."

"Well now you know how it feels
To be blatantly ignored."

"What the hell is going on, Jaliyah?
What are you trippin' for?"

"Jayson, it's late
And I told you I need sleep."

"Well I beg your pardon
Excuse the fuck out of me!"

With his last line
I powered off my phone
I had no idea
If I would ever go home

The rain was pounding hard
So, I didn't hear Sebastian come in

He inquired, "Are you okay?
I thought I heard you yelling
Was it a bad dream?"

There was that smell again
It had to be his cologne

"Are you okay? You're just staring."

"I'm sorry, I'm fine, Sebastian
I was lost in my thoughts."

"Okay, if you say so
But you seem a bit overwrought
Would you like more wood on your fire?
The temperature is dropping with the rain."

"Yes, please and thank you."

"I'll get it. Promise I won't disturb you again."

CHAPTER 2

LaRhonda N. Felton

Sebastian

<u>A welcomed distraction or a fleeting attraction?</u>

I don't know what she's going through
And I refuse to ask her again
Let me get the log for her fire
Either way, she's leaving in the morning
This job pays me very well
And her dad is a highly respected man
She thinks she's in my way
And she refuses to comprehend
I have been here for eight months
She has been a welcomed surprise
She's so pretty, gorgeous actually
I can't even lie

Her dad mentioned she's taken
And I won't overstep
But it seems there's trouble in paradise
And her dude is about to get left
He can't be much of a man
Letting her roam around alone
I swear brothers these days
Be living in the twilight zone
Don't know a good thing
If it bit them in the ass
And then throw a whole bitch fit
When the woman leaves him in the past

I know from experience
I haven't always done right
I was a royal asshole
According to my ex-wife
Truth be told, my ex is right
I had a hell of a lot to learn
Love comes with conditions
And respect must be fully earned
I know something's up though

Because I heard her yell
Her energy is so aggravated
In her mind, she's hiding it well
And maybe she does
For those that never pay attention
But she clammed up real tight
And I only made mention
I knocked on her door
I didn't want to just barge in

"Jaliyah, I have your logs
Why are you crying?"

"It's nothing, Sebastian
Just a lot on my mind
Thanks for the logs
I'll be just fine."

"Look, you don't know me
And again, I'm not trying to pry
But I've never seen *nothing*
Make a grown woman cry
Let me know if you need anything
I'll be in my room
And with any good luck
This rain will stop soon."

"I sure hope so
I'm leaving at first light
Besides, I'll probably be awake
The rest of the night."

"You don't have to rush off
Stay as long as you'd like
If you want, we can chat a while
Will that be alright?"

She asked, "Why did you take this job
Out here in the middle of nowhere?"

LaRhonda N. Felton

"It's a complicated story
But unlike you, I'll share
Mind if I take a seat?"

"No", she replied, pointing to a chair
You can cop a squat
Right over there."

She had stopped crying
And wiped her nose
I took a seat, looked at her
Ready to share, "Here goes
I took this job
To clear my head
I went through a nasty divorce
And this is where my spirit led."

"How long were you married?
If you don't mind me asking."

"For ten years
I don't know how it lasted
I didn't treat her right
I was unfaithful, the whole nine
But she kept giving me chances
Took me back every time
And that honestly
Was of no help
Because I was selfish
I only cared about myself
Seven years in
She filed for divorce
I begged her to come back
And she gave in, of course
I went right back to my old tricks
I really messed up
And just when I was ready to do right
She'd already had enough

She wouldn't talk to me
She was done with my shit
She filed for divorce a second time
And I couldn't talk her out of it."

"Wow, that's sad
Did you two have any kids?"

"No, but you know what
I almost wish we did."

"Why is that
Wouldn't that be worse?"

"I might've been able to convince her
To put the kids' needs first
But it's water under the bridge
My actions made my marriage end
And I'm happy now that
We can at least be friends."

LaRhonda N. Felton

Jaliyah

A needed distraction or a call to action?

"I don't think I could do it
Stay with a man that cheated
It's selfish and unnecessary."
I hoped I didn't sound too heated…

"Why didn't you let her go?
When she filed the first time
Clearly being faithful
Wasn't even on your mind."

"I loved her
It's that simple and plain
And I felt like I meant it
Saying I wouldn't cheat again."

"So, what made you cheat
And why couldn't you keep your promise?
Did you think you wouldn't get caught?
Come on, be honest."

"My word is all I have
And I cheated, but I never lied
I did what a lot of guys do
Having a wife at home and women on the side."

"Wow, your response is crass
Did you even learn a lesson?"

"Absolutely I did
My testimony became my blessing
Because while I was doing my dirt
She earned a degree
To recognize all the bells and whistles
On how to avoid guys like me

She and I had a long conversation
Just the other day
About certain men that approach her
And she's not even looking their way."

"Do you think you two could
Ever get back together?"

"I used to hope so
But now I know better
Which is why
I've been working on me
Dealing with the necessary growth
And putting into action the prayer of serenity."

"Does my dad know what happened?
Between you and your ex-wife?"

"He does, and he had some great advice
On how to improve my life
Your dad is a smart man
And he's taken me under his wing
But truth be told
My own father told me the same things
It's weird though, coming from my dad
It felt like do as I say, not as I do
But coming from your father
It's been a guide on how to push through
Getting past my own shit
To see the damage I caused
To heal my own traumas
And if it's too much, to take a long pause
Refresh and regroup, see things through a different lens
To grow and become an example
To be better than I was back then
I'm not there yet
But I'm working hard every day
I don't ever want another woman
Hurt by me in any way."

LaRhonda N. Felton

I was looking at the fire
Seemingly lost in space

I replied to him, "Yeah
My dad is great in that way
He always has a different perspective
He has a gift, an ability to see both sides
I think I'll lie back down now
I had a tiresome ride."

"Well, I will head back to my room
Hopefully, you can get some rest
When it rains like this,
Sleep is always the best."

"Good night, Sebastian
And thanks again."

"Good night, Jaliyah
See you in the morning."

Sebastian

<u>Opened and closed. My testimony, my role.</u>

It felt good
Owning my truth
She was the first woman
I'd ever opened up to
Without holding back
Ignoring fear of judgment
I admitted my mistakes
It's what adults do

I got back to my room
Listening to the rain pour
Thunder in the distance
I couldn't sleep anymore
I turned on the TV
Checked ESPN
I couldn't help wondering
What had Jaliyah crying
Her dad mentioned she was a writer
Yet she was very quiet
She keeps saying it's nothing
But my instincts aren't buying it

I gazed out the window
Seeing my own reflection
Missing what I didn't respect
Feeling immense sadness and rejection
Something I've never felt
Vulnerable enough to confess
But who knows what will happen?
I may surprise myself

Jayson

Bikes, cheating and lies… the truth can't be disguised.

I called Charae
To see if she'd heard from her friend
But she hadn't heard from Jaliyah since early this morning
She tried to get me to come back
Since Jaliyah wasn't home
I told her I was chillin'
Until I could find out what's going on
Jaliyah's been trippin'
Ever since I got that damn bike
Saying my priorities were out of order
Hell, maybe she's right

I need to get my shit together
And do better by my girl
My ass been slipping lately
But Jaliyah is my world
I'm in a situation though
I fucked up bad
And if Jaliyah finds out
She's going to kill my ass

Charae is her best friend
And we secretly hooked up
She threatened to snitch
So for the moment, I'm stuck
Shit has been off
With me and Jaliyah for a while
I can't even tell her what's wrong
'Cause this shit is just vile

I knew better
And I accept my part
The two people she trusted most
Are out here breaking her heart
I called her phone again

It went straight to voicemail
I didn't know what was up
And only time would tell

Jaliyah

<u>Emotionally drained and exposed pain.</u>

As I lay there in bed
Listening as it rained
I couldn't stop the tears that fell
Reliving my emotional pain

Jayson and Charae?
Cheating behind my back
Not even Sebastian's philandering ways
Seemed to top that

My dad will be livid
And he will have a lot to say
I couldn't stress on that now
I had too much on my plate
I needed to know for sure
If I was pregnant or just stressed
I didn't need any fuel for this fire
My life was already a hot mess

I watched the flames flicker
Until I felt hypnotized
I decided to try and fall asleep
Just one more time
I needed a clear head
To decide what to do
My life was too unstable
A fact I'm not used to

CHAPTER 3

LaRhonda N. Felton

Jayson

<u>Waking up alone just feels wrong.</u>

The sun is up
Jaliyah's still not at home
It was pissing me off
Being left alone
She was always here
Waiting for me
And somehow, I felt a shift
Like she was cheating

Could it be true?
After all this time
She found another man
And was no longer mine
No, I was tripping
She loved me too much
And even though I was wrong
She wouldn't give up
Not on us
And what we had
We would weather this storm
And I would win over her dad

I looked at my phone
A missed call from Charae
I wasn't calling her ass back
Nope, not today

The Cabin

Jaliyah

Breakfast skipped for yet another road trip.

It was 6AM
According to the clock
I slept a few hours
But the rain hadn't stopped
I needed to get on the road
I called my GYN instead
I was nervous about the outcome
But I needed to be prepared

Just my luck
She had a cancellation
She could see me in the morning
I scheduled without hesitation
I had more text messages
From both Jayson and Charae
I texted them both back
Saying I would be home later today

I invited Charae over
To clear the air
No need putting it off
She said she'd be there
Jayson didn't go to work
Claims he was worried about me
He needed to be concerned with himself
And get to packing
I woke up with a new mindset
To take care of this mess
And prayed harder than ever
For a negative pregnancy test

I put my clothes back on
And was headed to my car
Sebastian was coming up the hall

LaRhonda N. Felton

"Oh Jaliyah, there you are
I knocked earlier
I thought you were still asleep
You didn't say anything
Were you leaving without saying goodbye to me?"

"I'm sorry, Sebastian
I didn't realize you were awake
I was just going to sneak out
Since we were up so late."

"I'm an early riser
No matter when I go to bed
Before getting on the road
Join me for breakfast instead."

"I should really get going
I have a busy day planned
I need to get home
I hope you understand."

"I do, Jaliyah,
I won't stand in your way
It's very wet out
So, you be safe
But do me a favor
Call or text me when you get home
Here's my number
I will worry with you traveling alone."

"Thank you so much
For being my safe haven
And being kind to me
Even though I was a bit abrasive."

"Think nothing of it
It gave me something to do
Made the place less quiet
Having someone to talk to

The Cabin

If you need another escape
You know where to find me."

I gave him a hug
And then turned to leave
I was on the road about an hour
And my dad was calling

"Baby Girl, are you okay?
Sebastian said it was storming
I thought you were staying longer
I woke up to find out you left
I'm worried about you out there
Riding all by yourself."

"I'm sorry for causing you to worry
But, Daddy, I'm fine
I drive myself everywhere
And I do it all the time."

"I know you do baby
But even you must admit
Something is off
Just driving doesn't explain it
Now I won't pressure you,
But you're still my baby girl
And you and your mama
Are all I have in this world
You say the word
If you need me for anything
And I will be there
On the first thing smoking."

"I know that, Daddy
And I love you so much
I have some things to work out
But I will be in touch."

LaRhonda N. Felton

"Okay, Baby Girl, you be safe
And keep your doors locked
I will be awaiting your call
And don't make any unnecessary stops
All those country roads
Take a while getting to the interstate
I will call back in an hour
Answer my call, don't make me wait."

"Of course, I will answer
You're my dad
I'm watching my speed
And it's not raining that bad."

The Cabin

Sebastian

<u>When it rains it pours, but when it storms be warned.</u>

I thought she would've stayed longer
At least have a bite to eat
But she seemed determined
To leave in a hurry
Jaliyah's dad, Malcolm, had called
Almost as soon as she left
I had no choice but to tell him
It was storming and she was by herself

I hoped she was okay
And that she would call or text
I was getting another call
Damn, what's next?

I answered my cell
To the sobs of my ex-wife
She eventually explained
That her father had died
I called Malcolm back
And explained a few delays
That I would be with Bianca's family
For the next few days
Confirming he understood
That family comes first
And to extend his condolences
Because he knew how that hurt

I told him some deliveries
Would arrive while I'm away
He told me not to worry
To get to my family and be safe
I packed a bag
And locked the cabin down
Leaving everything secure
While I was out of town

LaRhonda N. Felton

I was glad she called
That she wanted me
Even if it was a sad occasion
Filled with grief
Being there for her
Was the least I could do
Especially after all the shit
I put her through

The Cabin

Jaliyah

<u>Secrets, lies and two people I now despise.</u>

I arrived at home
And saw Jayson's motorcycle in the yard
I sat there for a few minutes
Because this conversation would be hard

I called Sebastian
I got his voicemail
I may never see him again
Only time would tell
I called my dad
He answered on the first ring

"Dad I'm home now
You can stop worrying."

"That will never stop, my darling
One day you'll see
As soon as you become
A parent like me."

He had no idea
The sting his words had
Because if I were pregnant
It was over with my child's dad

Dad was going on and on
"Yes, we parents worry all the time
If you're eating right
If all is well when you respond with, *Fine*
Are you being treated well?
I mean it never ends
We go from being your protector
To competing to be your friend
It's a fine line my dear
Trying not to hover

And then an entirely different issue
Explaining why you aren't speaking to your mother."

"Dad, it's not that serious
But she's so quick to judge."

"I know, but it wouldn't hurt
To show her some love
Life isn't forever
And it's over in the blink of an eye
Just try to avoid the pitfall
Of regrets and wondering why
I know you just got home
So, my nagging is complete
But give your mama a call, okay?
Will you do that for me?"

He knew saying those words
Would get me every time
I'd do almost anything for my daddy
That was the bottom line

"Okay, Daddy, you have my word
I will call her this weekend
But I'm going inside now
To shower and do some sleeping."

"Baby Girl, you been in the car
All this time?
See what I mean
About that *Everything's fine*?"

"Daddy, we will talk soon
I won't keep insisting all is okay
Just trust me for now
I will get through today."

"I hear the words
But I can tell they aren't true
But I will do what you ask
And try to trust you
I love you, darling
Call me if you need
I will be right there,
You can trust and believe."

Jayson came to the door
"Are you coming in today?"

I grabbed my purse
"I'm on my way."

"I have been up all night
Wondering where you could be
Then you finally answer
Only to hang up on me."

I walked past him into the house
And started the shower
"We'll talk when I get out
Give me an hour."

"An hour? Is that all
That's nothing since you've been gone all night
Boy if that had been me
We'd be having one hell of a fight."

I ignored his comments
Because a fight was sure to commence
As soon as Charae got here
And I explained the reason for my absence

"Jaliyah, do you hear me
Or you don't feel you need to explain
I want to know where you were last night
And I'm not asking again."

LaRhonda N. Felton

"First of all
I don't answer to you
I am a grown ass woman
Missing me is something you should get used to."

"What the hell does that mean?"

"It means exactly how it sounds
Let me go shower
And then I will expound."

He went into the kitchen
I stepped into the tub
The water was nice and hot
It felt really good
I let the water cascade around me
Camouflaging my tears
My emotions so raw
I hadn't cried that much in years

While drying off
I heard my phone chime
A text message reminding me
Of my appointment tomorrow at nine

CHAPTER 4

LaRhonda N. Felton

Sebastian

<u>Evil personified. A weaker man may have cried.</u>

I arrived at my ex in-laws house
And Bianca was a wreck
I can't remember the last time
I'd seen her so upset
Her dad's passing happened so suddenly

He had been washing the car
When her mom came out
And found him lying in the yard
The paramedics came
But there wasn't anything they could do

"Sebastian, I'm glad you're here."

"You knew I'd come for you."

Her mom, Delores, interjected, "Now isn't that funny
You couldn't keep your dick in your pants
But now it's anything for you?
Bianca, don't be a fool and give him another chance
He dogged you out long enough
Worried me and your daddy sick."

"Mama, now is not the time
Would you just stop it?
I wanted Sebastian to come
To be here for both of us
No need to be so mean
Bianca crying, yelled, "Enough is enough!"

"I'm sorry, Bianca, but I can't
I won't turn the other cheek
I don't know where you got that weak shit from
But you didn't learn it from me."

"No, Mama, I'm not weak
And we are nothing alike
I don't believe in emasculating a man
All for the sake of being right."

"Maybe if you had
He'd still be home
But you gave that dog too much freedom
Allowing him to roam."

"Goodbye, Mama, I'm leaving."

"Remember Bianca, keep your knees locked
You don't know where he's been
And you haven't had your flea shots."

Damn, did I drive all this way
To be disrespected and dismissed?
I came two seconds from telling Delores
Exactly what she could kiss
That woman was something else
Evil on two legs
My ex father-in-law may finally have peace
Now that he's, unfortunately, dead

LaRhonda N. Felton

Jaliyah

I'm sorry my ass. I'm leaving the past in the past.

I got out of the shower
And began to pack
I'd decided after my appointment
I wasn't coming back
It didn't matter the outcome
I could write anywhere
And pregnant or not
I was on the road from there

I heard the doorbell ring
Charae yelling, "Hey it's me
Is the food done?
Because I'm ready to eat."

I closed my room door
And hit the lock
I needed to get it together
And for the tears to stop
I threw in toiletries
Whatever I might need
Anything I didn't have
I would be replacing

"Jaliyah", she called
Come on out friend."

"I will be there in a minute."

I got angry then
Friend my ass
You don't have a clue
A real friend would never
Do the shit that you do

The Cabin

I opened my room door
For this dreaded conversation
I sent up a silent prayer
And proceeded without hesitation

The air was thick
And Jayson looked afraid
Well he damn well should be
With the way I've been betrayed

Charae pointed out, "I thought you were cooking."

I stated, "Let's all have a seat
With what's on my mind
You won't want anything to eat."

She replied, "Well damn, boo
What's on your mind?"

"The fact that you two
Have been fucking and lying."

For a few seconds
There were crickets
And the guilt so evident
You couldn't miss it
I expected one or both of them
To tell me I was lying
I guess I was hype for nothing
I looked at Jayson and he was crying

He asked, "Can we talk about this alone?
Just you and me?"

"What explanation do you have, Jayson?"

"Can I just talk to you please?"

LaRhonda N. Felton

"Charae, why so quiet?
Don't you have something to say?
You advising me to leave him
'Cause you fucking him anyway!"

She grabbed her purse
"Please tell me you aren't leaving
Without saying a word
Explain this to me
After all we've been through
Who made the first move?
Somebody needs to say something
That's the least one of you can do."

Charae snapped, "This is where I exit
Because this isn't my mess."

"The hell it's not
You need to check yourself
I went to your house yesterday
To find his motorcycle in your yard
One of y'all need to say something
I put that on God
I am trying to keep my cool
And not blow the fuck up
But y'all both on mute
Is too damn much!"

"Baby, please, Just let her go
She isn't your friend. She always been a ho."

Charae challenged, "Oh yeah?
I'm the pimp, you the trick
Because for the past six months
I been financing that dick
Tell the whole truth
Don't just throw me under the bus
You needed money
You were paid amply to fuck."

I looked from him to her
And asked, "What the fuck is really going on?"

Charae reported, "Sorry ass lost his job
Now I'm going home."

I looked at Jayson
"What the hell does she mean?"

Jayson appealed, "I wanted to tell you
Baby, please forgive me."

Charae looked back in the door
"Oh, and Jayson drop off my keys
I'll be at the house
Don't forget the motorcycle please."

I advised, "You can go with her
For you and me, this is the fucking end!"

"So, I don't get a chance to explain?"

"Explain what? Why you were fucking my friend?"

LaRhonda N. Felton

Jayson

<u>No excuses. Explanation useless.</u>

"Listen if you let me talk
It's not that cut and dry."

"Alright I'm listening
"Explain yourself. Give it the old college try."

"I did lose my job
But she was on me months before that."

"Just exactly how long has it been
You two have been fucking behind my back?"

"No, that's not what I'm saying."

"What the fuck is it then?"

"Well if I could speak
Without you interrupting…"

"I'm zipping my lips
So, get to the point, 'cause telling me more lies
Isn't what you want."

"Ever since your party
Charae has been on a mission
Hell, even the night of
She groped me in the kitchen
Now she played it off
Saying she was buzzed
She thought I was someone else
And I believed that's what it was
But I started paying attention
Watching her closely
And anytime you would leave the room
Her eyes were always on me."

"Why didn't you say something?
Let me in on the truth."

"I never thought it would go this far
At least it wasn't supposed to
Charae saw me downtown one day
Dropping off my résumé
She popped up out of nowhere
Claiming she saw me and wanted to say *Hey*
She asked why I wasn't at work
And initially I didn't tell her the truth
The last thing I needed was
Her to blab the shit to you
I had a plan
To do that in my own time
Once I found another job
I knew everything would be fine
But Charae wouldn't let up
She kept on pressing
Saying she was my friend too
And she could tell I was stressing
So, I told her I lost my job
And she said she understood
If I needed her to float me a loan
To simply ask and she would
So, I took her up on her offer
I had bills to pay
And I didn't think anything of it
Since we were friends anyway
Things with you and I
Started to fall apart
Because I was stressed the fuck out
About finding a job
Your daddy made it plain
That I needed to man up
And I didn't want you going to him
Trying to take care of us."

"Jayson, get to the point
And explain to me
How in the hell did this
Lead to you cheating?"

"Charae called me over
Supposedly she needed furniture moved
And she would take money off the loan
I had no idea it was in her bedroom
I get over there to help
And she wasn't even dressed
I decided I would wait outside
Then she laughed and admitted, 'I confess
I don't have anything for you to move
But I can pay more bills
Just have sex with me
And we have a deal
Jaliyah will never know
You will be getting paid
And you can still pretend
To go to work every day'
She begged me 'Jayson let me show you
I only want to fuck
Ever since the night of the party
I've fantasized about it so much
You don't have anything to lose
It's like the best of both worlds
You get to keep the love of your life
And also fuck her girl."

The Cabin

Sebastian

<u>Same old place, yet a different space.</u>

I followed Bianca back to our old place
And I will admit it initially felt strange
Being back in a space
I never thought I'd see again
It felt oddly unfamiliar
Like I didn't belong
The house I was in, no longer my own
I felt like a stranger in her home

I put my things in the guest room
I asked Bianca had she eaten
She responded she couldn't
The same answer with sleeping
So here I am back in my old kitchen
It looked the same
I made a pot of soup
Just like I used to, nothing had changed

Bianca came in the kitchen
"Sebastian, I apologize
My mom was out of line
She's still very angry, and just needs more time."

"I have no issue with her anger
I guess it's the timing of it all
I came here because you asked me to
I could tell you needed me when you called."

"So, you wouldn't have come otherwise?
To at least pay your respects?
After all he was your ex father-in-law."

"Keyword in that sentence is ex."

But that's beside the point
I didn't realize her emotions were still so raw
Bianca assumed, "I think it's everything
The situation overall."

"Has she expressed to you
Her anger with me?
Because I could've come straight here
My presence didn't need to be so unsettling."

"Of course she did
But that was a while back
I didn't think with my father's passing
She would still go off like that
Thank you for coming
I know you didn't have to."

"To be totally honest, Bianca
It felt like the right thing to do
Have the services been arranged?"

"Yes, my dad took care of everything
He knew what he wanted
He left no room for disagreeing
Day after tomorrow
We say our final goodbyes."

I held her in my arms
As she began to cry

CHAPTER 5

LaRhonda N. Felton

Jaliyah

<ins>The loss of a friend, as my new normal begins.</ins>

I was floored
I didn't know what to say
Was I really supposed to believe this shit?
I needed to talk to Charae

I pulled up to Charae's
With Jayson close behind
She was going to talk to me
There was no leaving this time
I waved at her neighbor
Since I knew he was watching
Or at least his cameras were
With no intention of stopping

I rang her doorbell
Even though I had a key
I wouldn't use it
This visit was far from friendly
Charae opened the door

"Me walking out wasn't enough?
Now you coming to my house
With all this dramatic stuff."

"You can't be serious
Thinking I would just go away
We are hashing this out
And it's happening today."

I pushed my way in the door

"What the fuck, Charae? I thought we were friends
The least you can do is talk to me
After all, it is my man you been fucking."

Jayson came inside and lashed out, "Tell her
Don't even try to lie
Tell her how you been coming for me
This whole damn time
How you got me over here
Bribing me with gifts and shit."

Charae clapped back, "Your slimy ass accepted
You never had to take any of it
I tried you, Jayson,
But you could've said no anytime."

"My question for you Charae
Is why you trying a man of mine?
With all the people you could've fucked over
Why me?
And then give bullshit advice
Knowing the reality."

"I don't know, Jaliyah,
Maybe you told me too much
And I began wondering
What he would be like to fuck
I never intended for it to happen
But I found out he needed cash
And it was triflin' I know
But he also had an option to pass."

"You know what Charae
That's a fact I can't deny
He made a choice
You both did
To cheat and to lie
And am I to understand correctly
That the motorcycle was a gift from you?"

"It was a conditional gift
But he's lost that too."

LaRhonda N. Felton

Jayson yelled, "Fuck you, Charae!
Jaliyah, baby, I'm sorry."

"No, no it's way too late
To come with an apology
You both fucked up
And in a major way
This is the last time
I will allow myself to be played
By a triflin' ass man
And a skank ho of a friend."

I slapped Charae's face

"Bitch don't ever call me again
As for you Jayson
You have two hours to pack
Don't make me call my daddy
Cause you don't want any parts of Malcolm Black
He has been waiting
Impatiently I might add
To have the smallest reason
To get on your ass."

"Jaliyah, wait please
Can I at least get a ride back to the house?"

I swung my purse
And hit him in the mouth
The chain from the strap
Cut him in the face
I left him inside
Bleeding all over her place

The Cabin

Jayson

<u>Today is a bitch. I could've stayed in bed for this shit.</u>

I went in Charae's bathroom
And cleaned my face
I called my boy to pick me up
To take me back to my place
Well what used to be my place

Charae offered, "Jayson you can stay here
We're not sneaking around anymore
Everything is in the clear."

"Charae, are you delusional?
The love of my life just left
And all you can think about
Is your own fucking self."

"You weren't thinking about the love of your life
When you were between my legs."

"Yeah, you're right
Makes me wonder what's wrong with my head."

She touched my dick

"Semi hard as always, I see
Stop being stubborn, Jayson,
And stay here with me."

I pushed her hand away

"Charae, keep your hands off my dick
The last time we fucked
Was the last time, I mean it
What the fuck was I thinking?
Sleeping with the likes of you
Jaliyah should be mad as hell

LaRhonda N. Felton

I'm fucking mad at me too
I should've just told her
I should've come clean
Instead of listening to you
Plotting a fucking scheme."

"Fuck you, Jayson,
Hell, I didn't twist your arm
You were a willing participant…"

I heard my boy's car alarm

"Charae lose my fucking number
I never want to see you again."

"Jayson don't say never
You just might be back beggin'."

"Beg you?"
I laughed, "Bitch please
If I let you suck me off right now
You'd be on your knees."

"Is that what you want?
Will that make you stay?"

"Hell, fuck no
You ain't that good at it anyway."

With that statement
I headed to the front door

"Charae lose my number
Don't call me no fucking more."

I went outside
And got in the car
I was mad and hurt
And I had played a part

The Cabin

My boy asked what happened
I explained all my shit
Sweat was burning that scratch
And it hurt like a bitch
Chris drove in silence
Before saying, "Man that was stupid
Fucking your girl's best friend?"

"Yeah, advice this late man is useless."

"Don't shoot the messenger!"
"I know dawg, you're right
Is it okay if I crash at your place?
For a few nights."

"Yeah bro that's cool
You can have the couch
'Cause I know your ass can't
Stay at Jaliyah's house."

"Naw man I can't
She put my ass in the wind
And rightfully so
I should've never fucked her friend."

LaRhonda N. Felton

Sebastian

<u>Damned if you do, damned if you don't.</u>
<u>Life rarely gives you everything you want.</u>

I woke up the next morning
To a note from Bianca
Letting me know
She'd gone to check on her mama
I was debating this whole time
If I should leave or stay
I didn't need my presence
Getting in the way
The death of a loved one
Causes enough stress
I didn't need my being here
Making anyone more upset
I would wait it out for now
And let the events play out
I looked at my phone
To see what the
Voicemail was about

It was Jaliyah
Letting me know she'd made it home
It was good she left when she did
She didn't need to be at the cabin alone
The place is secure
It's just so isolated
Made for privacy and comfort
Too much silence can drive you crazy
I got up and made breakfast
Called and checked on my dad
He said I needed to come for a visit
My mom missed me something bad
I told him it would be soon
I missed them too
And keeping in touch more
Is what I intended to do

The Cabin

I've taken too much for granted
And sometimes it's a crisis
To harshly remind me
How short life is
I spent a lot of years
Being selfish thinking of only me
I'm a constant work in progress
Embracing my growing masculinity
Becoming the man
That my dad raised
I've always known better
But I enjoyed when I misbehaved
I'm learning though
My antics caused hurt and pain
For some whose respect
I may never regain
The only thing I could do
Is ask for forgiveness and try to rebuild the trust
If not, then my sincerest apology
Would need to be enough

LaRhonda N. Felton

Jaliyah

<u>Changes in life and changes in love…
Changing what is into what was.</u>

I went back to the house
Placed my packed bags in the car
Scheduled a locksmith because I knew
Jayson wouldn't be too far
I was praying about this appointment
I wanted to cut all ties
Didn't need a baby connecting me
To a man I despised
Just like clockwork
I heard a car in the driveway
He needed to pack his shit quick
Because I didn't have anything to say

He came in the door
I saw the scratch on his face
I felt a twinge of regret
But anger was quick to take its place

"Jaliyah, I know you must hate me
This was never my intention
I know I fucked up
Even giving her my attention
You don't have to say anything
Maybe one day you'll accept my apology
Just know from the deepest part of my heart
Baby I am so, so sorry."

I saw tears stream down his face
But I couldn't say anything
My love was replaced with hate
His presence alone
Disgusted me
And all I wanted him to do
Was get his shit and leave

The Cabin

Love… a four-letter word
That was constantly misused
By people who didn't feel anything
Until they knew they were about to lose

He confessed, "I'm done talking
And I will leave you in peace
Just know you're the love of my life
And you always will be."

LaRhonda N. Felton

Sebastian

Grief, regrets and forgiveness.
Somehow, we will get through this.

Bianca came in the door
She looked so tired
Her eyes were swollen and red
From the constant crying

"How is your mom?" I asked.

"About the same as yesterday
Inconsolable about my dad
Yet finding room for hate."

"I guess that hate is directed at me
I can leave, Bianca, if you feel that's best
The last thing I ever want
Is to pile on more stress."

"No", she refuted
"I want you to stay
My mom promised to be civil
She will stay out of your way
I told her if I could forgive you
She should at least try
You aren't who you used to be
You've truly become a different guy
And even though what we had is over
We're better off as friends
You deserve to say goodbye too
In my dad's eyes, you were forgiven."

"Thank you for telling me that
I hate I never got to apologize
And contrary to my past behavior
I cared about how I looked in his eyes

My dad raised me right
And I chose to stray
Bianca, I regret what I did to you
Each and every day."

"I forgave you, Sebastian,
A long time ago
I know a lot of your antics
Came down to your ego
You're a good-looking man
That has a way with the girls
Tied down to one woman
Slowed down your world
Don't get me wrong
I was angry for a while
But I got past it
And reclaimed my smile."

"I'm glad to hear that
Maybe you should take a nap
Tomorrow will be a heavy day
Just know I'm here for you
I have your back."

CHAPTER 6

LaRhonda N. Felton

Jaliyah

<u>Tests and questions, and hard life lessons.</u>

Jayson got his shit and left
The locksmith was waiting for me
I was paying time and a half for the trip
Since I told them it was an emergency
He changed out my locks
And gave my new key
I locked my door, went in my room
And cried myself to sleep

I woke to my alarm blaring
And I had a headache from hell
I showered and dressed for my appointment
To take a test I prayed to fail
I needed negative results
So I could move on with my life
No matter the outcome
I'm going back to the cabin tonight

I arrived at my appointment
Thirty minutes ahead of time
The receptionist seemed to pick up
That I had a lot on my mind
I did the usual validated insurance
Confirmed my address
It wouldn't be long now
I could take this dreaded test

"Ms. Black", the nurse called
"How are you?" the usual small talk
I was so nervous about the outcome
I could hardly walk
Got my weight checked
And given that awful little cup
It wouldn't be long
Before I knew what was up

The Cabin

The nurse asked,
"Any issues you want to address?"

"I basically came in
To take a pregnancy test."

Answered the last menstrual question
As well as those about sex
The nurse completed her questionnaire
And advised the doctor would be in next
She gave me the robe
Telling me to leave it open in front
I sat on the table with that noisy white paper
Praying I would be blessed with what I want

Sebastian

<u>Saying goodbye is always sad.</u>
<u>I couldn't imagine the pain of losing my dad.</u>

My ex father-in-law's funeral
Was one of the worst in my life
I wished I could do more
To comfort my ex-wife
She was beyond consolable
And consumed with grief
I came in and took some medicine
I needed immediate headache relief

Bianca stayed at her mom's
After the repass
And I won't lie, after it was over
I immediately hauled ass
I didn't want a minute alone
With my ex mother-in-law
I didn't want to hear her
Wretched mouth at all
I packed my things
To hit the road in the morning
Those headache pills
Had me sleepy and yawning
I sent a text to Mr. Black
To let him know what I was planning
That by the weekend
I would be back at the cabin

The Cabin

Jaliyah

<u>Impatiently waiting, nerves deteriorating.</u>

"Ms. Black", the doctor called
While knocking on the door
My *Come in,* was barely audible
As my heart hit the floor

"Your pregnancy test didn't yield a result
So, we will need to draw blood for another test
Blood will show the pregnancy hormone
And an ultrasound, if needed, will be next."

"How long would I need to wait
For the blood test to come back?"

"Oh, not too long
We have a lab here
So, three to four hours max."

"So, I will find out today?
Because I'm quite anxious to know."

"Then let me get the nurse back in here
No need to wait around anymore."

The nurse came back and drew blood
By then I was ready to leave
As I grabbed my purse, my phone chimed
Jayson was calling me
I sent him to voicemail
Once I got the results back
I was changing my cell number
As a matter of fucking fact

I went to breakfast
And shopped a little bit

LaRhonda N. Felton

Waiting for the doctor's call
I couldn't focus on shit
The phone store would be my last stop
Before I hit the road
I did a bit of damage in the mall
Heading back to the car with my bags in tow

I heard my name being called
I turned and Jayson was on his way
I didn't have time for this
Especially not today

"What the hell, Jayson?
Are you following me?"

"No, Jaliyah, I'm not
I'm not crazy
I had an interview
With a company across the street
I came over here after that
To get something to eat
Do you think we can talk?"

"Jayson I'm all talked out
We said everything last night
There's nothing left to talk about."

"Jaliyah, to be honest
I have a lot left to say
I know I was wrong
Please just listen, babe."

"Jayson look, it's over now
And maybe that's for the best
We haven't been happy for a while
We've been living in a familiar mess."

"*Familiar mess?* You can't be serious
We weren't that bad

I know we have something special
If I could have one more chance."

"Jayson, stop please
I need space and time
To process what I've been through
And attempt to clear my mind."

My cell phone chimed.

"Jayson, I'm sorry, but I need to go
As I walked away
I answered the doctor's call, "Hello?"

Jayson

Her trust is broken. I'm left wishing and hoping.

Damn! She got in her car
And was driving away
I didn't get a chance to
Say half of what I wanted to say
I really needed to
Make her see
How sorry I am
Ask her to forgive me
I didn't sleep all night
Thinking of her and this interview
I didn't even get to mention
That I'd been offered the job too
It wouldn't be long
Until I was back on my feet
I needed to let her know that
Maybe then, she would come back to me
My boy told me
I could stay longer if needed
I'm glad I had a timeline now
Of when I would be leaving
Jaliyah was my world
I had to regain her trust
I strategized on how to get her back
While I waited for the city bus

The Cabin

Sebastian

<u>Hurt can mend and you can be friends.</u>

Bianca knocked on the room door
"Mind if I come in?"
"Sure, come on
I'm just finishing my packing."

"You leaving, so soon?"

"Yeah, I left in the middle of a project
I need to get back and finish up
Then decide what I want to do next."

"Thank you, Sebastian,
For dropping everything to be here."

I looked at Bianca
Her eyes were full of tears

"Are you going to be okay?"

"I will", she sighed, "although I don't know when
I'm staying at my mom's tonight
So, she's not alone again."

"That's a good idea
I think you both need time and space
To adjust to a new normal
And it may help more if I'm not in this place."

"What time are you leaving?"

"Before the sun comes up
Avoid some of the rush hour."

"Sebastian, will you keep in touch?"

"Of course, I will, Bianca
I'm happy we can now be friends."

"Safe travels tomorrow
Please call me when you get in."

The Cabin

Jaliyah

<u>Oh what tangled web we weave, when we slip up and conceive.</u>

The nurse informed me, "Jaliyah
Your results are in
We can see you at two."

"I can be there in ten."

"Are you sure?
We close for lunch in fifteen minutes tops."

"That means I need to hurry
And I don't have time to talk."

I made it back to their office
After running a red light or two
No traffic cameras mounted
No violations to prove
The doctor was waiting
With my results in hand

"Ms. Black, you can sit."

"No, I prefer to stand."

She chuckled and shared,
"I had the lab run the test twice
You are not pregnant
You should sleep easier tonight."

I inquired, "But my period is late
Is there something else wrong?"

"Yes, Jaliyah, the stress you've put on yourself
Is wreaking havoc on your hormones
With proper rest
Diet and exercise

You should level out in a month or so
You will be just fine
If anything, else comes up
Call and we'll get you in
But this is all stress induced
Get some rest girlfriend."

"Thank you, Dr. Hayes."

"You're welcome. Enjoy your day
Oh, and before I forget
Here's the ultrasound for Charae
I know you two are like sisters
And she wanted you to conceal
The sex of her baby
Until her gender reveal."

What the fuck?

I rapidly blinked my eyes
And swiftly fixed my face
Trying to hide my surprise

"Pardon me, Dr. Hayes,
Are you sure she wanted you to give this to me?"

"Yes, those were her instructions
After her appointment last week
Her pregnancy was a shock
Took the news a while to sink in
I can see you're alarmed as well
But you'll be there for your friend."

I couldn't say a word
After yesterday's events
Am I supposed to keep her secret?
Ain't this a bitch!

The Cabin

"Well dear, I'm heading to lunch
I have a surgery scheduled this afternoon
Jaliyah, call if you need me
And I'll see you soon."

I walked back to my car
Feeling some kind of way
To find out Jayson was having a baby
Not with me, but Charae.

CHAPTER 7

LaRhonda N. Felton

Jayson

<u>Constant bus ride and running out of time.</u>

I got on the bus
And called Jaliyah again
It hurt like hell
She wasn't answering
Her silence is justified
With the way I behaved
She deserves better
And my karma was making me pay

I see the pain in her eyes
When she looks at me
But if I give her too much time
There's no chance of us reconciling

I need her to know
How sorry I am
I want to prove to her
I can be a better man
I'm not giving up
I'm going to stay on my grind
And prove to her we belong together
That she should be mine

The Cabin

Jaliyah

<u>Isolation and a much-needed vacation.</u>

I stopped by the phone store
Got a new cell and a number change
Once I got to the cabin
I would sync my contacts again
I got some groceries
And a few things I would need
Because it would be a while
Before anyone would see me

I was going off the grid
To get my mind and body right
Enjoy some peace and quiet
Take some time and write
I got on the road
While the music played
I was lost in my thoughts
What a hell of a day
I decided I would email Jayson
He deserved to know
That Charae was pregnant
Even if she didn't think so

I guess she never thought
I would actually find out
Smiling in my face
Sitting up in my house
Her pregnancy should've been
The most amazing news
But the last forty-eight hours
Have delivered quite the bruise

I almost cursed out loud
When Dr. Hayes gave me the envelope
But I didn't bring her into this bullshit
She didn't need to know

My prayers had been answered
No pregnancy for me
I could cut all ties to Jayson
Live my life peacefully

I got to the cabin
And everything looked dark
I thought Sebastian would be here
He was gone, which was odd

I unpacked my car
And locked myself inside
It was a little spooky being here alone
A fact I couldn't hide
I called my dad
He needed my new number anyway

He answered, "Hey Baby Girl
Is everything okay?
I called an hour or so ago
And couldn't reach your line."

"I have a new number, Daddy
But everything is just fine."

"No, not quite, something is up
You are riding around alone again late at night
Now a new number
Something isn't right."

"Okay, Daddy, I will be honest
Some things have changed, that's true
I kept it to myself because
I didn't want to burden you."

"Listen, you're my daughter
You and your mama are all I've got
You let me decide
If I feel burdened or not."

"You're right, Daddy
But I needed to handle this on my own."

"Well what is all this you're referring to?
Get to talking, come on
Jayson and I broke up."

"God heard my cry!
Wait, I'm sorry sweetheart
You two broke up? Why?"

"I know you weren't a fan of Jayson's
And it bothered me that you two were never friends
But maybe it was for the best
Considering how it came to an end."

"Baby Girl, he was okay
Just not good enough for you
I didn't trust his fickleness
His lack of follow through
When I met your mama
I changed my life
I set goals and kept them
Because I wanted Jacquelyn as my wife
I knew I needed to prepare
To take on her needs as well as my own
To be the man my father raised me to be
Or leave that woman alone
I emulated my father
By taking care of my wife
But I also followed my mother
In loving your mama for life

Jacquelyn's never had to worry
Or want for a thing
I'm not perfect by any means
But it's not from lack of trying

So, if me wanting the best for you
Means boycotting Jayson
I will take up my picket sign and march
Without regret or hesitation
Tell me what happened
How did he lose you?
Because without you in his life
He won't know what to do."

"He cheated on me, Daddy"
I said between sobs
I didn't realize saying it
Out loud would be so hard
"He cheated on *me*
With my best friend no less."

"Wait a minute, let me get your mama
She needs to hear this mess."

"Please no, Daddy, not now
I can't take her ridicule
Her condescension sometimes
Makes me feel like a fool."
"Baby Girl, you and your mama
Must fix this
Using me as your go between
Is downright ridiculous."

"I know, Daddy
Just, please not today
And the icing on the cake
Jayson is having a baby with Charae!"

"That son of a bitch!
I will kick his ass,"
I heard my mom say in the background
"Charae never did have any class."

The Cabin

My dad confessed
"Hey baby, I didn't hear you come in."

My mom chuckled, "I guess not
You're too busy gossipin'."

"Talking with my baby girl
Is never ever gossip
It's necessary conversation
Discussing life's topics."

My mom laughed
"Jaliyah, call me sometime
I am your mama
And I miss you, Sunshine."

I was listening and thinking to myself
Who is this coming through the line?
It sounded like my mother
I couldn't remember the last time she called me Sunshine

"Sure, Mom
I will give you a ring."

"Good," she snickered, "I'm going to make dinner now
Before your father claims he's starving."

I laughed with dad another hour or so
I never mentioned to him that I wasn't at home
For fear he would throw a tantrum
About me being at the cabin alone
I needed the peace and quiet
Even if it wasn't part of the plan
I was still curious though
On the whereabouts of Sebastian

LaRhonda N. Felton

Sebastian

__Guilt gifts aren't all meaningless.__

Bianca went back to her mom's
And I had the house to myself
I was too wired to sleep
So, I assembled her new shelf
She would never ask me to do it
But I know she could use my help
The last thing she needed
Was to worry about something else
It was after three in the morning

By the time I was done
The shelf came with directions
But it was a difficult one
I should just hit the road
I couldn't sleep anyway
And leaving now I would avoid
The morning rush on the interstate

I sent Bianca a text
And locked up the house
Got in my truck
And headed down south
Back to the cabin
And peaceful serenity
It was just too bad
Jaliyah wouldn't be there with me

The Cabin

Jayson

<u>Moving up, wish me luck.</u>

My boy was happy for me
I told him I got the job
I wanted to tell Jaliyah
Her ignoring my calls made that hard
I checked out some apartments
First thing was to get off this couch
Get my finances in order
And get out my boy's house
I appreciated him
Giving me a place to stay
But to get Jaliyah back
I must make my own way
Grow up and be the man she needs
Handle business and be responsible
I had a long road ahead of me
But it was not impossible
I called Jaliyah again
Her number was out of service
I guess she changed it
And that made me nervous

I wanted her back so bad
And it seemed that may not ever be
I couldn't accept that it was over
An overwhelming sadness settled upon me
The only woman in the world for me
And I broke her heart
Her dad always said I wasn't good enough
He didn't trust me from the start
My phone buzzed
Jaliyah sent me an email
A picture of a sonogram

Charae's? What the hell?

LaRhonda N. Felton

Jaliyah

<u>Shampoos and emails, they could both go to hell.</u>

I woke up hungry
But I felt refreshed
I slept very deep
To have been here by myself
I checked the clock
And it was after nine
I couldn't believe I'd been asleep
All that time

I decided to shower
Before I eat
The steam from the bathroom
Would create some heat
I slept under three blankets
I was still a little cold
But not cold enough
To want to go home
I would make sure today
To get some logs for a fire
It was close to dark yesterday
And I was too tired
I sent Jayson an email
Letting him know he was going to be a father
I almost emailed Charae
But I figured why bother
That was their fiasco
And I wanted no parts
Other than to be left alone
Working on a fresh start

This past week had dealt a massive blow
Practically blew up my life
You can fool me once
It's a choice if I let it happen twice
I got out of bed

The Cabin

No need for regrets
I was good to Jayson
And he wasn't ready yet
Maybe he never will be
My dad always said we wouldn't last
And he was right, again
Jayson had now become part of my past
We enjoyed some great times
And some not so great too
Cheating with my best friend
Is something I would've never thought he'd do

I turned on the shower
No cap since I was washing my hair
Turned on the radio
To put good energy in the air
I grabbed my shampoo and conditioner
And got in the tub
I wished I'd changed the station
Ugh, the radio segment was all about love

LaRhonda N. Felton

Sebastian

<u>Fruity shampoo and feet that won't move.</u>

Traffic was a lot smoother
Than I had anticipated
I was about ten minutes from the cabin
I found myself elated
It was half past nine
And I was starving
Too close to home
And I wasn't stopping
I wanted a steak for dinner
And a dark red wine
Baked potato and broccoli
Would complement my meal just fine

Cereal, bacon, and fruit for breakfast
Chill today and get a little rest
Maybe call my therapist and schedule a session
I could use it after paying my respects

I pulled onto the road for the cabin
Everything looked like I left it
Being back here alone
Was a little quieter than I expected
I opened the door
Something felt off
I heard music up the hall
Then suddenly someone coughed
When I spoke with Malcolm earlier
He didn't mention anyone being here
I grabbed the fireplace poker
They were leaving and that was clear
I tipped quietly up the hall
Using my tactical training
Pain is what I would inflict
By this ass whooping I was bringing

The Cabin

I eased the door open and stopped
Slid the poker in the leg of my sweatpants
Did Jaliyah come back?
I didn't see her car
I couldn't risk the chance
I smelled fruity body wash or something
This person had to be female
And before I knew it
My dick was hard as hell
I wanted to open the door
But my brain and my feet were confused

She opened the bathroom door
Screaming, "What are you doing in my room?"

"I didn't know you were here."

She dropped her shampoo to reach for a robe
And I didn't think it was possible
My dick got harder than it was before
I tried to leave
But the poker fell in my shoe

"I'm sorry, Jaliyah
I didn't know it was you."

She laughed a bit
"I'm sorry, I didn't know you were back either
But I'm glad you are
Can you please fix the heater?"

Then I laughed
With my back to her
"There's a tech coming tomorrow
I see roughing it isn't for girly girls."

We both laughed and I could finally move
"I'll be back, let me go
Unpack in my room."

CHAPTER 8

LaRhonda N. Felton

Jaliyah

__Birthday suits and shadows. I had him rattled.__

Oops, I had no idea
Sebastian was in my room
I didn't know where he'd been
Or that he would be back so soon
The five o'clock shadow
Made him look even better
I took a seat in the chair
I needed to get myself together
Him seeing me naked
Wasn't part of the plan
Honestly I wasn't bothered
He was so fine, damn
I hoped he was happy I'm back
Because I was excited
And he liked what he saw
His sweatpants couldn't hide it
I laughed to myself
Being here will be fun
He couldn't move for staring
What have I done?

The Cabin

Sebastian

<u>Personal questions and a few confessions.</u>

I made it to my room
Damn Jaliyah is fine
Seeing her naked
I almost lost my mind
I sat on the side of the bed
As the blood flow returned to my brain
I would subtly find out
How long she was staying

I unpacked my stuff
And grabbed a quick shower
I smelled food cooking
Shockingly, I'd been in there an hour
Doing what I had to do
To take the edge off
I could see me making love to her
She looked so damn soft

This was a job for me
Malcolm's daughter was not a perk
But her in this cabin
Was going to make it much harder to work

I went to the kitchen
And she made me a plate

"I fixed us brunch
Too early for lunch and for breakfast too late."

"Thank you, Jaliyah,
What a welcome surprise."

I couldn't help noticing
The robe barely covered her thighs

LaRhonda N. Felton

Silky smooth
And chocolate brown
Damn this was going to be hard
With her hanging around

"So, what brings you back this way?"

"Too much turmoil in my personal life."

"Where were you?"

"I went to see my ex-wife."

Was that sigh one of disappointment?

"Oh," she replied
I couldn't read her mind
But my response surprised her this time

She paused a while before asking
"Is everything okay?"

"No, it's not
We buried her father yesterday."

Jaliyah's eyes softened
"Wow I'm sorry to hear that
I couldn't imagine my life
Without Malcolm Black."

"Life is short
And I definitely agree
My dad and I are close as well
He means a lot to me."

We both sat quietly
And devoured our food
I changed the subject
Death was ruining my mood

"So, tell me, Ms. Black
How long will you be here?"

"Indefinitely, Sebastian."

That was music to my ears

Jaliyah

<u>A familiar heat making it hard to keep my seat.</u>

Damn sitting across from him
Gave me naughty ideas
He had me picturing things
I hadn't thought of in years
Jayson was good in bed
But he wasn't a freak
I'd had to tone down my wild side
When we started dating
But I saw something different
Looking into Sebastian's eyes
And I felt a familiar heat
Begin to simmer between my thighs

"Jaliyah, you okay?
You seem to be miles away."

I smiled and replied,
"Absolutely, just enjoying the day."

Jayson

<u>Regrets and voicemails. My life has become a living hell.</u>

I called Charae
My call went straight to voicemail

"Charae, you need to call me back
What in the whole hell?"

I know she better not be pregnant
How the fuck did Jaliyah know before me?
Emailing the sonogram
Charae and her fucking secrecy
I hate the day I got in bed with her
I feel so fucking stupid
I would never get Jaliyah back
If this was what my truth is
I hate that I got caught up
And lost the person I loved most
If Charae is playing games
Her ass was going to be toast

LaRhonda N. Felton

Sebastian

Grilling, chilling and acknowledging deeper feelings.

Seven weeks had passed with Jaliyah here
And the sexual tension was building
I went to bed most nights
With a hard on pointing at the ceiling
We shared cooking duties
And the household chores
I was growing accustomed to her being here
Loving her essence even more
She still hadn't shared
What made her return
I decided I would ask again
Since it was so much more about her to learn

I was cooking dinner tonight
I decided to grill
Some salmon steaks and corn
I had the wine ready to chill
She was making dessert
Which was a banana split
And she was going to tell me what happened
I insisted on it

I let the cat out of the bag to her dad
That she had come back
He said she didn't tell him
But he wasn't upset about that
He mentioned she needed a break
Something about issues with her ex
That he was glad it was over
But he didn't elaborate on the rest
I wanted specifics
And maybe it wasn't my place
But we were here together
With each other every day

I know she's feeling me
I could see it in her eyes
The way she talked and looked at me
It was just a matter of time
I didn't want to get involved
If she still had feelings for her ex
Even if it was just a night
Filled with passionate sex
I felt a strong connection to her
In this short length of time
And I wasn't into games anymore
Especially not with this heart of mine

LaRhonda N. Felton

Jaliyah

<u>Brazen glances and second chances.</u>

Being here with Sebastian
Felt so comfortable and new
Watching him take care of this place
Gave me something to look forward to
He was simply amazing
And open about his life
He told me all about Bianca
And how horribly he'd treated his ex-wife

He was in therapy
Getting his life together
He practiced meditation
And he worked out no matter the weather
I lay in bed alone at night
And wondered if he sleeps naked
I masturbated to mental images of him
Until I couldn't take it
We were both walking on eggshells
The sexual tension was thick
And I kept taking glances
At his sweatpants print
But trusting a man again
I was nowhere near ready
For a night of sexual passion
The thought alone made me hot and sweaty

I looked outside
Saw him prepping the grill
Damn he was so fine
With his kiss the chef apron on and I will
Kiss him everywhere
Nice and slow
And when he begged me to stop
Kiss him some more

He saw me watching
He looked up and waved
When Ms. Kitty jumped
I told her, "Hush girl, behave."

LaRhonda N. Felton

Sebastian

<u>Internal desires burn hotter than a roaring fire.</u>

She was watching me
And she had been for a while
She played a naughty game
And I'm a man, not a child
I'm not sure what she's used to
In a man or a lover
But I delivered in the bedroom
Like no other

I had no inhibitions
And an insatiable libido
I knew what I could do to a woman
And that inflated my ego
I waved her outside
So, she could get a better view
She liked watching me
And I loved looking at her too
Especially how her hips swayed
Under the tiny robes she wore
Made me remember walking in on her
And wanting to do more

The memory of her naked and wet
Was etched in my brain
Which could've possibly
Drove a weaker man insane
But I was stealth in my maneuver
I wanted no doubts in her mind
That when the time came
She would beg to be mine

The Cabin

Jayson

<u>Soul food, lonely blues and strange dudes.</u>

I love my new job
I've been there a few weeks
I still hadn't heard from Charae
She took forever getting back to me
I stopped by her place
But she hadn't been there
I saw her neighbor looking
His nosey ass was creepy as hell
I emailed Jaliyah about that sonogram
And she was slow to reply
She may not give a damn anymore
I hated it, but I understood why

I drove past our old place
To check the mailbox
But I couldn't access it
Apparently, Jaliyah changed the locks
I had no way to contact her
Other than email
And I wanted to talk to her
Everyone's missing. What the hell?
I was so desperate
I almost called Mr. Black
But I knew he would be satisfied
And I wasn't ready for that

I'm keeping my nose to the grind
Learning this new job
And I will admit
Not having Jaliyah has been hard
She was my cheerleader
She saw the best in me
And she pushed me to want more
I can only blame my stupidity

LaRhonda N. Felton

I decided to stop and pick up dinner
Soul food is what I've wanted all day
I walked in the restaurant door and in the corner
I saw trifling ass Charae
Only thing is she hadn't seen me
She was at the table talking with some dude
I sat in the cut and observed the exchange
Decided not to approach yet; I didn't want to be rude
They were having a full-on argument
She tried to touch him, and he slapped her hand away
I wondered to myself
What's really going on with Charae?

The Cabin

Jaliyah

<u>Healthy conversations, brimming with necessary revelations.</u>

Sebastian brought the last of dinner inside
I had the table set
I sat across from him
Unprepared for what came next

"So, Jaliyah, tell me
What really brought you here that first night?
I've been open and honest with you
About every aspect of my life
Haven't I gained your trust?
To share with me a little piece
I mean we've been here together
The better part of seven weeks."

"Wow! Sebastian
I didn't see that coming
I guess you have a point
I should share something."

I saw relief come across his face
He wasn't sure how I would react
But he had been honest with me
And I admired him for that
I told him everything
From beginning to end
Right down to the unborn child
Jayson was having with my former friend
I told him about my pregnancy scare
And how I was truly relieved
When I found out there wouldn't be anything
Tying Jayson to me
I admitted something to him
That I didn't even admit to myself
That I was embarrassed by the fact
Jayson could be turned on by someone else

LaRhonda N. Felton

Women have egos too
When it comes to the desires of her man
And it's a huge blow to accept
That he's satisfied in another woman's hands

Sebastian countered, "Wait, Jaliyah
It's not quite that cut and dry
Each woman brings out something different
In every single guy
Now don't get me wrong
What they did was fucked up
But simply because they messed around
Doesn't make her better than you, trust
She was easier than you
Meaning her expectations weren't as high
She didn't add the pressure
With her, he didn't have to try
With you, it was a constant audition
That was easy to recast
Because he wasn't bringing anything to the table
Not anything that would last
He didn't feel good enough
Like he never measured up
And here's your friend down for whatever
She was an easy fuck
Most women don't realize
Until it's way too late
That they do too much for the wrong man
That they shouldn't even give the time of day
And to a man like I once was
It's like blood in the water beckoning the sharks
We skillfully seek out and devour
A giving and loving heart
And it's not done intentionally
But sometimes we can be savage and all out for self
We fuck up and move on
Leaving the cleanup for someone else

The Cabin

I used to be Jayson
And not that long ago
I was turned on by the conquest
But that's not me anymore
Therapy has helped me realize
The damage I caused
So, when I meet women now
It's not all about the drawers
I want to get to know her
And what truly makes her tick
Not just how good her mouth would feel
Wrapped around my dick
I don't mean to sound so crude
But we're both grown
And that honestly used to be me
A dog looking to bury my bone."

"Thanks for your honesty, Sebastian,
And for giving me a safe space
For a while I wasn't sure how to process it
My head was all over the place."

"Jaliyah, you're a good woman
And I haven't known you very long
But I can guarantee you
Jayson regrets doing you wrong."

My eyes filled with tears
Because I knew he was right
"You mind cleaning the kitchen?
I'm calling it a night."

"I don't mind at all
Let me know if you need anything."

I couldn't even respond
For fear of bursting out crying
I thought I was past this phase
The hurtful part, the random tears

LaRhonda N. Felton

Talking about it felt good at first
But it also made me realize my biggest fear
Being alone
Never finding the love I deserve
The person to share my life with
Life really threw me one hell of a curve
I showered and lit my favorite candle
A soft scented cashmere
I heard a knock on my door
Before I placed the earbuds in my ears

Sebastian entered
"Hi, I brought your banana split
You need something sweet
You deserve it."

Sebastian paused
"Mind if I join you?"
I replied, "Stay please
I would love for you to."

I gave him an ear bud
As Sade began to sing
We ate dessert quietly
Not saying much of anything

Apparently, we were both tired
And at some point, drifted off to sleep
I woke up at five in the morning
With Sebastian asleep beside me
He was a very attractive man
Dark hair and thick brows
I couldn't stare too long
Because I wanted to kiss him right now
I turned over slowly
So as not to disturb his sleep
And he did the weirdest thing
Wrapped his arm around me
He whispered groggily

The Cabin

His breath in my hair

"Didn't your parents ever tell you
It's impolite to stare?"

I loved the huskiness of his morning voice

"I didn't know you were awake."

"I didn't mean to fall asleep in here
I hope that's okay."

I relaxed in his arms
"To be honest I'm glad you stayed
I was in my feelings
And didn't want to be alone anyway."

"Sade serenaded us to sleep
She did and at some point, my phone died."

He smelled simply amazing
Wrapped in his embrace I closed my eyes
Before I knew it
I was asleep again
The next time I woke up
It was well after ten
I felt a little sad
Finding myself alone
I wanted to wake in his arms
Where I felt completely safe and warm

Sebastian

Running scared, to clear my head.

I had to get out of there
Out of Jaliyah's bed
She had no idea of the naughty thoughts
Running through my head
I wanted to make love to her
But I knew she wasn't ready yet
Last night talking about Jayson
She was visibly upset
She is a beautiful woman
I loved her body in my arms
I wanted to protect her
And keep her safe from harm
After she fell asleep
I found it hard to go back
I wanted her sexually
But like I said, she's not ready for that
I got out of bed
Went for a run
Came back to the cabin
And got some work done
I had a Skype meeting
With my therapist at noon
I decided to make breakfast
Because Jaliyah would be up soon

CHAPTER 9

LaRhonda N. Felton

Jayson

<u>Confusion, marriage and a baby carriage.</u>

I watched the exchange a bit longer
Between dude and Charae
Placed my order
Before walking over to speak, "Hey"
Charae's eyes were as big as saucers
I asked her point blank
"Is it mine or is it his daughter?"

Dude looked at her
Then looked at me
I snatched her keys from the table
I declared, "Oh no, you're not leaving
I've called you repeatedly
And it's time you explain
This is real life Charae
Quit with the fucking games."

I guess I was a little loud
I saw folks look in our direction
I slid in the booth beside her
"Talk", I demanded, "Don't keep us guessing."

Dude looked from her to me
And he stated, "I don't have time for this shit
My wife is blowing up my phone
Having a damn conniption fit."

He insisted, "Rae you need to fix this
I already have a kid as it is
Go on and take the paternity test
It's a possibility your kid is his
You knew what time it was
We were friends with benefits
Now you pregnant and whatnot
I am not with this shit

Look, holla later or whenever
I got to go
If it turns out to be mine
Then we can go to court."

With that, old boy got up
Grabbed his jacket and left
I looked at Charae and implored

"Please explain yourself."

She was on the verge of tears
I passed her a napkin

"Charae, you need to talk to me
Tell me what's really happening
Jaliyah emails me a sonogram
With your name attached
You not returning my calls
What's up with that?"

"Look Jayson, I'm sorry
A lot is going on", she uttered in tears
I'm not sure yet if the baby
Is yours or his."

I wondered, "Are there any others
That need to throw their hats in the ring?
Don't look at me like I'm crazy
Shit, it's a question that anyone would be asking
When can we find out?
Because everyone needs to know."

She replied, "It's a risky process
But we can find out while the baby's in utero."

"How far along are you
Why didn't you tell me?

This is a major life changing event
That shouldn't be entered into lightly
But like everything else
You had to have your way
Damn how anyone else feels
Or what they have to say
Just know this Charae
I'm filing for joint custody if the baby is mine
I refuse to let you improperly influence
My child's mind
You have done some foul shit
Seemingly with no remorse
I guess we all had it coming
And must let karma run its course
I will be in touch."

I got up to leave
"I can't believe you were so low down
To keep something like this from me."

I grabbed my order
And walked out the door
No way Jaliyah would take me back now
That thought hurt me to my core

I was about to get in my Lyft
When Charae pulled beside me
"Jayson, come with me
I can drop you where you're going."

I took her offer
Because it was vital for her to explain
Why she kept this secret
She needed to stop playing this dangerous game

She cried, "Jayson, I'm sorry
I didn't mean to keep this from you
But from the second I found out
I wasn't sure what to do

The Cabin

I didn't know Jaliyah was on to us
Not that I ever wanted her to know
But once she did
I wanted us to give a relationship a go."

"Did you ever think that was possible?
With how low down it began
I mean even I see the messiness
Everything about us was sleazy and trifling."

"You have a point
And I never planned for any of this."

"No, I completely disagree
You only thought of yourself, downright selfish."

"Damn, Jayson, I wasn't alone
You were there too."

"You're right, I was
Let's not forget the other dude
By the way, did you know he was married?"

"Not at first, but then so what
All men are dogs anyway
I've been cheated on too much."

"Damn, Charae, I didn't see it until now
You are bitter and scorned
You're angry about your past
And taking it out on everyone
Jaliyah was just collateral damage
You know she didn't deserve that shit."

"Damn, Jayson, okay!
How long are you going to harp on it?
Why is it you could never care for me
You light up just saying her name."

LaRhonda N. Felton

"To put it bluntly, Charae,
You two are not the same
Jaliyah would've never done
The shit we did to her behind her back."

She pulled over and admitted
"I never thought of it like that
But at the same time, Jaliyah isn't perfect
Don't get shit twisted
She's done her dirt too
And you just dismiss it."

"I know she isn't perfect
But she's never betrayed you
Or even me for that matter
Don't use imperfection as an excuse
We *fucked* up
In an extremely major way
She didn't deserve it
I regret this shit every day."

Charae conceded, "She hates me"
I agreed, "She hates us both
But we can't even be mad
She is angry, and justifiably so."

Charae started crying
This time her grief seemed sincere

She sobbed, "I can't believe I lost my friend
She's been my sister all these years
I never meant to hurt her
Honestly, I was jealous
Of what you two shared
I have been so selfish
And now what's supposed to be
One of the happiest times of my life
It's one of the worst
Because of my scheming and lying

Can we ever fix this?
I need my friend."

"I don't know, Charae,
I won't even pretend
She's not responding
But she hasn't blocked my emails yet
Maybe give her some more time
We owe her at least that."

Charae began driving again
The rest of the ride was quiet
She promised to keep me updated on the baby
I muttered, "Okay", but I didn't fully buy it.

LaRhonda N. Felton

Jaliyah

<u>Confused feelings and a hurt that leaves me reeling.</u>

I smelled coffee and bacon
Sebastian was back
I was feeling some kind of way
With him just leaving like that
I didn't say anything
Tried to play it cool
But eventually I would ask him
What made him leave my room

I went into the kitchen
He had prepared a mini feast
, "Gosh, Sebastian, this is a lot
Too much for just you and I to eat."
He replied, "I know, the landscapers are coming
To put in the fountain your dad talked about
I thought breakfast would be nice
Since I won't be around to help them out."

"Oh, are you leaving?
No just a therapy session on Skype
Oh, by the way do you have
Any ideas on dinner tonight?"

"None actually
Did you have anything in mind?"

"I will come up with something
We have nothing but time."

"Thank you for breakfast
I guess I'll write a while today
I surely don't need to be
In the landscaper's way."

The Cabin

"They will be in and out most of the day
Hopefully, it's a one-day job
I chuckled, "Getting them to work after this breakfast
That will be the hard part."

He laughed sheepishly,
"Is there anything else you need?
"No, but thank you, Sebastian."
I turned to leave

I went to my room
And pulled out my laptop
More emails from Jayson
I wish he would stop

Oh no! Her too?
I see an email from Charae
Well she signed up for it
And I got time today
I opened her email first
She began with an apology
Yeah, yeah what else slut?
I already know you're sorry

I kept on reading
She's not sure who her baby belongs to
Apparently, it wasn't just Jayson
She was also fucking some married dude
I lost all respect for her
She didn't give a damn
Him being mine, yours
Or the next woman's man

I have never in life
Wanted the man of a friend
We can talk, laugh and joke
But that's where it ends

LaRhonda N. Felton

Jayson's first three emails
All begging me to call
Telling me he needed to get his mail
I deleted it all

I submitted a change of address online
He shouldn't have anything in my mailbox
His mail has been going to his mother's
Ever since I changed the locks
He didn't seem to understand
There was no coming back
I decided to reply to his last email
To tell him just that

Jayson look
I understand our breakup has been rough
But you must realize
You can't keep this up
I've requested to be left alone
And I've asked for some time
You betrayed me in the worst way possible
Cheating with my so-called best friend and lying
Things will never be the same
There's no need to try
I wish you the best
With everything in life
As for your mail
Check with your mom
I put in a change of address for you
When I moved on
If you're in contact with Charae
The same rules apply
I wish you both a nice life
Good luck and goodbye

I hit send
And closed my laptop
I went to get a cold drink
Suddenly I was extremely hot

The Cabin

It was twelve-thirty
I figured the workers would be outside
I turned the corner to the kitchen
And stubbed my toe so hard I almost cried
I heard this voice

"Oh shit, my bad are you okay?"

"I am so sorry
I didn't know anyone was coming this way."

Reaching for my toe
I began to stumble
And from my mouth
The curse words tumbled

"Shit! Fuck! Ouch! Fuck!
What the hell is on the floor?"

"It's my toolbox, ma'am
I put it down to prop the door
Sebastian said it was a cooler in here
That he filled with drinks
I came in and put it down
I didn't even think
Let me help you
Guide you to a seat
And I will get some ice
To put on your feet."

This guy scooped me in his arms
Much to my surprise
And when he turned around
I was staring right into Sebastian's eyes

CHAPTER 10

LaRhonda N. Felton

Sebastian

<u>Intrusive strangers and shocking anger.</u>

"Excuse me, Mike, what is going on?
Homie, you can put her down right there."

I walked ahead of him
And pulled out the chair

"It's not what it looks like, Sebastian,
She stubbed her toe
I was just being gentlemanly
Helping her out, you know
I'm terribly sorry
I didn't think when I put my tools down
I never intended for her to get hurt
I didn't know anyone else was around."

Jaliyah was sitting there
Looking from him to me
By the look on her face
Her toe was really hurting

I yelled, "Who's here and who's not
Isn't ever your concern, Mike,
What is it you were looking for?
Everything you all need is out back."

Mike answered, "My bad, Sebastian,
I thought the cooler was inside
I'm so sorry she got hurt."

Jaliyah interjected, "It's not a big deal, I'll be fine."

I was mad as hell

I stated, "Mike, I will handle it from here."

The Cabin

He grabbed his toolbox
And uttered, "I'm sorry again my dear."

I looked at Jaliyah
She responded, "Thanks", and nodded her head
I don't know why I was so pissed
Shouldn't I just be grateful instead?

I put ice in a towel
And had Jaliyah wiggle her toe
It was good and swollen
But didn't appear to be broke

"Sebastian, it wasn't his fault
That guy felt so bad."

"Yeah, but you got hurt on my watch
How am I to explain that to your dad?"

"That accidents happen
And people make mistakes
And that my toe hurts like a son-of-a-bitch
But I'll eventually be okay."

I looked at her
And shook my head

"I'm just glad you're not hurt too bad
Or Malcolm might want me dead
Can you stand?
Or apply any pressure on your toe
She stood up and winced in pain
I will take that as a no."

I carried her back to her room

"Maybe elevating it will help a little bit
If your dad knew about this
He would have a fit."

"But he doesn't have to know
He doesn't even know I'm here."

Sebastian's eyes were wide
He was looking weird

"Yeah, he does know
He's known for a few weeks
I didn't realize you being here
Was to be kept between you and me."

"It's no big deal
I just hadn't told him yet."

"Next time, I promise to ask first
Pardon my disrespect."

The Cabin

Jaliyah

<u>Hunger or pain? Limping to the door, hunger wins again.</u>

Damn my toe hurt
And taking a shower was a bitch
Sebastian kept checking on me
And bringing me ice for it
I took some ibuprofen
And a long afternoon nap
I woke up starving
And got up to get a snack
I was limping to the kitchen
Paying attention this time
I couldn't spare another injury
I would most assuredly be crying

Sebastian came in the front door

"Jaliyah, what are you doing out of bed?"

"I came for something to eat."

He replied, "I didn't cook, I got takeout instead
A few of the landscapers will be back tomorrow
To finish up their work
I must go for supplies, you can tag along
That way you won't get hurt."

I looked at him and laughed

"I will go
Because I need things myself
Not because I hurt my toe
How was your therapy session?
You never mentioned how it went."

"Seeing him carrying you
Caused me to forget."

"Sebastian, are you still on that?
Let it go
He was only trying to help me
After I hurt my toe."

"Jaliyah, you don't know men
The way that I do
You think it's innocent, he's salivating
Getting a feel and enjoying the view
You were wearing a tank top
And some itty-bitty shorts
Him touching you like that
Made my blood boil."

"And why is that?
Why did you get so mad?"

He went into the kitchen
Seems he didn't want to answer that

The Cabin

Sebastian

<u>**First moves, who knew?**</u>

I couldn't answer her question
But she was right, I was mad
Was it because I saw her in his arms?
I didn't hide my disdain as well as I thought I had
Maybe it was time I confess
And tell the truth
Let Jaliyah know I liked her
Because I truly do

I took our food out
Arranged it on two plates
I was going to let her know how I feel
Sooner than later, no need to wait
I went back into the living room
To find Jaliyah gone
I went down the hall to her room
I wasn't eating alone

"Jaliyah," I called
Before opening her door
And when she answered, "Come in."
My mouth fell to the floor
She had scented candles lit
Smelling of Jasmine and cashmere
I stuttered when I probed
"Wha-What's going on here?"

Her voice seductive, "Well, Sebastian
Someone had to make the first move
And I decided it might as well be me
Since it seemed much harder for you."

"To be honest I was done waiting
I planned to tell you tonight
Exactly how much I like you."

LaRhonda N. Felton

"Oh, is that right?
You walked away without
Answering my question
And you think I believe you?"

"Is that what you're expecting?
I've never lied to you Jaliyah
So, to answer you
Believe what I say
Is exactly what you should do
But you tell me
What is all of this?
What's on your mind?
What's with all these candles lit?"

"If I need to further explain
I may as well blow them out."

"No need for that
Just tell me
What this is all about
She responded "I'm giving you permission
To make love to me
Am I wrong to assume?
You weren't thinking the same thing?"

"I, I was…" I stammered
I couldn't believe she had me shook
I'm always overly confident
But she was giving me this look
Sexiness oozed from her
From her head to her swollen toe
I was more than a little curious
About what she had in store

And even though my curiosity
Had been thoroughly piqued

The Cabin

I wanted and needed to know
How she truly felt about me
I couldn't delve into
Another situation based on great sex
If that were the case, I wouldn't be in therapy
And I could've stayed married to my ex
Jaliyah was exciting, intelligent
And I felt we had a good chance
At something more
Than us just getting into each other's pants
The old me wouldn't give a damn
I would've already had her in the buck
But the old me didn't want a relationship
The old me only wanted to fuck
I knew I would need to word this
In a way that didn't hurt her feelings
I wasn't turning her down
But I needed to know she was healing
That she wanted something more
Not using me to get over Jayson
I could just dick her down
But I don't play the position of a rebound replacement

So, I asked her point blank
"Jaliyah, where do you see this going
Because I want more with you
Than just sex with the homie
Are you sure you're over Jayson?
And not just seeking sex
I'm looking for something real
And I feel that you and I connect."

She looked at me smiling
"Sebastian, ensuring my intentions aren't misread
I really like you and want more than you just in my bed
I am also looking for something deeper
A connection that lasts
I want to be deliriously happy with someone
I haven't experienced that in my past."

She then decided
"I tell you what
Let's not do this tonight."

I'm thinking *Damn, just my luck*
I had to appear unaffected
Since I was the one that posed the question

I smiled and replied, "Okay."
Sadly, agreeing with her suggestion

She confirmed, "It will happen
But more organically
No pressure on you
And none on me."

The Cabin

Jayson

<u>When some chapters close, they deal crushing blows.</u>

I got Jaliyah's email
And I guess I'd refused to realize
The finality of our relationship
We were done forever in her eyes
And that hurt me
I always thought I had a chance
To show her how much I loved her
And get another chance to be her man
Accepting what she wants
I won't bother her again
Maybe one day in the future
We could possibly be friends
I saw on the email
She copied Charae
I decided to call her
To check in and say *Hey*
She didn't answer
That was just as well
No need for a message
I hung up on her voicemail

LaRhonda N. Felton

Sebastian

<u>Surprise flowers and a much-needed hour.</u>

We ate dinner
But there was this awkward silence

She acknowledged, "Something feels off."

I whispered, "Let's try this."

I kissed her
Cupped her face in my hands
Her lips were so soft
Causing immediate reaction in my sweatpants
The kiss lingered
As we both almost lost control
And threw caution to the wind
Saved by an intrusive knock on the door

Jaliyah looked at me
"Expecting someone", she inquired?

It was a guy with flowers
"I have a delivery for Ms. Black."

I looked at her, she looked at me
"What the hell? This is odd."
She burst out laughing
As she read the card

At first, I was mad
And now I'm just hurt and sad
When did you start keeping secrets from your dad?

I laughed and admitted
"This one's on me
He wouldn't know you were here
Had I not spilled the beans."

The Cabin

"It's cool, I'm going to call him
And thank him for the flowers
Maybe then we can catch a movie?
Give me about an hour."

I needed that hour
To get rid of my erection
I made sure to add to my supply list
Boxes of protection

This hold out would be hell
And I didn't think we'd succeed
That kiss alone
Reminded me of my need
To feel a woman close
Breathe in her scent
Feel the softness of her body
My shirt was covered in her fragrance

I headed to my room
And started a cold shower
I needed to take this edge off
Until I was face-to-face with her again in an hour

CHAPTER 11

LaRhonda N. Felton

Jaliyah

<u>Conversations with daddy always make me happy.</u>

My dad answered the phone
Pretending to be in tears

He cried, "Oh it's my baby girl
I haven't heard from her in years."

I laughed at his jesting
"Daddy, come on you're exaggerating a bit
It hasn't been years
And you know it."

"It felt like it, Baby Girl
I kept waiting for your call
You're back at the cabin
And didn't tell me at all
I had to send flowers
To smoke you out of hiding."

I just kept laughing
"Daddy, you got me crying."

He laughed, "I missed you, my love
Have you been okay?
Are you resting well?
And enjoying your stay?"

"I am, Daddy
I'm taking it one day at a time."

"I am so glad Sebastian's there
And was able to ease my mind."

"It suddenly came to me
Why you two never met

The Cabin

You didn't come home that summer
Which in hindsight, was for the best
Sebastian wasn't mature then
And hadn't settled down
He might've broken your heart
And we wouldn't be friends right now
That summer Patryk and his family
Joined your mom and I at the cabin
You went to Jamaica with Charae
That's exactly what happened."

"I'm glad I didn't meet him then
He's so different now
But it had to be in the cards
For our paths to cross somehow."

"I'm sorry, Daddy
My intention was to let you know
I've just been clearing my mind
And taking things real slow."

"Good, you needed a break
And I'm grateful to know you aren't alone
If construction is too much at the cabin
You know you can always come home."

"Thanks, Daddy
But honestly, I'm fine
Sebastian's taking good care of me
And I'm enjoying the downtime."

"I'm sure he has
And that's good to know
You both have been through some things
On the rediscovery road."

I admitted, "He's shared a lot with me
You know, about his past
But what's your take on him Daddy?"

LaRhonda N. Felton

"I'm curious to know what makes you ask?"

"To be honest
There's an attraction between us
He's single, I'm single
You know two single adults."

"In my opinion, honey
He's become a stand-up guy
He trusted me with his secrets
And I've never questioned why
I felt if he wasn't trying to change
He wouldn't have brought it up
He was looking to clear his conscience
And he needed someone to trust
I'm glad he chose me
Because he didn't deserve to be judged
He asked for a listening ear
And that's exactly what I was."

"Daddy, you're amazing
You make time for everyone."

"For him it was easy
I love Sebastian like a son
People make mistakes
And deserve the benefit of the doubt
He's been on the up and up with me
Which is why I haven't had to come out."

The Cabin

Sebastian

<u>Movies, popcorn and places that are warm.</u>

I thought my shower
Would take the edge off
But I was still semi erect
Nowhere near soft
I put on my baggiest pajama bottoms
And a T-shirt
Splashed on a little cologne
Hell, it couldn't hurt

Jaliyah hadn't come out yet
I made some popcorn
Pulled out the FireStick
To see what's new on Amazon
She came up the hall
In a T-shirt to her knees
And what does she do
Sit down right next to me
The wine was open
And the movie selected
She smelled so good
I put my arms around her, I couldn't help it
She didn't shy away
Instead she snuggled in close
And then she literally
Brushed my neck with her nose

"Sebastian, you always smell good
Even when you come back from a run."

I smiled, "Thank you, Jaliyah,
Here's the popcorn if you want some."

"Is something wrong?
Do I make you nervous?" she inquired.

LaRhonda N. Felton

"Not at all", I lied.
Very matter of fact
"But I'm trying to be a gentleman
I don't want it to feel like I'm pressuring you."

"I don't feel that way at all
You're not doing anything I don't want you to."

I felt her tongue on my neck
As I turned and kissed her lips

I pleaded with her huskily,
"Jaliyah, are you sure you're ready for this?"

She answered me
By putting my hand between her thighs
She was so wet
But I wasn't surprised
I fingered her slowly
She rolled her hips to my stroke
I took her right to the edge
As her breath caught in her throat
I took off her shirt
And she was naked underneath
Her body was so beautiful
A sexy masterpiece
I positioned her body
In the corner of the couch
As I licked her all over
Making my way down south

I put deep kisses
On the inside of her thighs
Teasing her the whole time
I saw lust in her eyes

"Show me how bad you want it."

The Cabin

She put her hands on my head
And pushed my face
Between her legs
I gave her pretty pussy a kiss
I licked inside her lips
I gripped her hips tightly
As I gently sucked on her clit

She was squirming
Trying to loosen my grasp
But she couldn't get away
I had a tight grip on her ass
I alternated between licking and sucking
She was squeezing my head
Because she had to hold onto something

I flicked my tongue fast
Over her tiny clit
I knew this was driving her crazy
And then I sucked a little bit
She came hard
And she came fast
I teased her nipples
Making her orgasm last

She moaned out loud in ecstasy
Giving my ego a boost
Not that it was necessary
Because my beard was covered in her juice
I picked her up
And carried her to my bed
She was still feeling the effects
I felt the trembling in her legs
She looked so sexy
As she reached for me
Begging, "Sebastian
Make love to me please."

LaRhonda N. Felton

I did just that
Happy to oblige
I was engulfed in the warmth
Between her thighs
She was tight
Yet the perfect fit
Her body was tailor made for me
Designed with precise measurement

The Cabin

Jaliyah

Golf carts and heart drops.

I have never in my life
Had an orgasm that fast
Not that there were many
Lovers in my past
But this side of Sebastian
Was on a whole other level
No wonder his ex stayed so long
Leaving had to be the devil
He was inside of me
Penetrating my soul
It was like some missing part of me
Was finally whole
We were fused together
Like perfect pieces to a puzzle
I knew now for certain
Sebastian was like no other
He was kissing me
Filling me with intense passion
I think I was starving before
And lovers in the past had given me rations
My body responded to him
In synchronized motions
I was in pure sexual bliss
He was in tune and focused

He whispered, "Tell me how it feels
Are you being pleased?"

I spoke with my pussy
And gave his dick a squeeze

He groaned, "Yes baby
Don't stop, keep squeezing me like that
Show me just how good it feels."

LaRhonda N. Felton

As I rubbed his back
We made love on and off
Until the wee hours of the morning
And as crazy as it sounds
We both woke up horny
We made love again
Before heading out for supplies
We didn't have time to cook
So, I ordered breakfast for the landscape guys

I grabbed my purse
And got in my car
Sebastian said, "No baby I'll drive
I can't be cramped up; we need to drive too far."

I got out of my car
And followed him around the driveway
In the garage I saw a Toyota Tundra

"Now this is a surprise I must say."

"A surprise?" he asked
"Tell me why."

"You just don't seem like
A pick-up kind of guy."

He opened my door
And helped me inside
I must admit
It was a sweet ride
I remarked, "Wow
This truck is very nice."

"Thank you
I'm glad you like."

We shopped a few hours
Browsed a few stores

The Cabin

He looked at me and asked
"Are you good? How's your toe?"

"It feels a little tight
In this closed-in shoe."

"I tell you what
Here's what we'll do."

He was talking to the security guard
He drove up in a golf cart. "Hop in."

I questioned, "Where did you get this from?"

"I'm here all the time. Melvin and I are practically friends."

"Melvin the security guard?" I laughed so hard
But me hopping in wasn't debatable
Taking the pressure off my toe
I was extremely grateful

We talked, laughed, and ate a late lunch
It was an amazing day
Filled with an evening of lovemaking
And sexual play
I was insatiable
And we fell asleep in my bed

Sebastian woke me up at four
He lamented, "Bianca is dead."

I sat up quickly
And asked "What? What do you mean?"

"She committed suicide
Her mother just called me."

"Oh my gosh! I'm so sorry, Sebastian."

LaRhonda N. Felton

He looked like a deer in the headlights

"I will put on some coffee
Are you alright?"

He shook his head no
And no other words were spoken
I saw sadness in his eyes
He looked so heartbroken
I went into the kitchen
And sat as the coffee brewed
I didn't know what else to say
Or what I should do
I made him a cup
With a shot of Cognac
It would calm his nerves
And he could use that
I walked back into my room
And his face was full of tears
I wasn't sure how to respond
Or what I should do here
I put the coffee down
And pulled him close
He held onto me and cried
How long? Who knows?
The coffee was cold
But he seemed more settled

"What do you need me to do to make it better?"

He confirmed, "You're doing it
Allowing me to keep it real
Without judging me
I can be open to feel."

The Cabin

Sebastian

Permanent end. The unexpected loss of a friend.

I never expected that call
That Bianca was dead
I never knew she was struggling
She never once said
That she needed help
Or that things got that bad
I knew she hadn't fully gotten over
Losing her dad
But to take her own life
I just didn't think it would get that extreme
And even more shocking
Her mother called me
I'm so glad Jaliyah's here
And I'm not by myself
Being in her arms comforts me
Unlike anything else

I admitted, "I just had no idea
That Bianca was in such a bad way
I checked on her from time to time
But I didn't reach out every day
Why didn't I see it?
She was my ex-wife."

"Sebastian you couldn't know everything
You two no longer shared a life."

"You're right babe
But I feel so bad
Maybe I should've checked in more
After the loss of her dad
Her mom confirmed she'd get back to me
With information on the service
But being alone with her mother
Makes me a bit nervous."

LaRhonda N. Felton

Jaliyah

<u>Preparing for a flight and being alone for the night.</u>

The next few days
Were solemn and sad
Considering the circumstances
They weren't totally bad
Sebastian seemed more loving
As if that were possible
Bianca's service was tomorrow
Him getting along with her mother seemed implausible
He was flying in this time
Making it a one-day trip
I was driving him to the airport
And he was having a fit
About leaving me here alone
He wanted me to come with him
I didn't feel it was appropriate
No need to further anger the opposition
Bianca's mom was contrary enough
Based on her behavior the last time
And with Bianca not there to referee
Seeing me with him might blow her mind
It was just twenty-four hours
I told him I would be fine
I would lock everything down
And I promised to stay inside
He looked uneasy
Like he had more to say
But it was time to leave for the airport
So, we were on our way
He was quiet during the drive
I kept stroking his cheek
He kept his hand on my thigh
And continued to remind me
To double check the doors
And not to let anyone in

The Cabin

That maybe he should call my dad
I convinced him in the end
That I was an adult
I was there alone before
And I promised to FaceTime with him
To show him all the locked doors
I kissed him at the airport
And practically pushed him to the plane
He had the nerve to contemplate
The possibility of staying

CHAPTER 12

LaRhonda N. Felton

Sebastian

<u>Away from home without my phone.</u>

I didn't want to leave
But I got on my flight
Maybe it was the circumstances
Something just didn't feel right
As soon as I touched down
I was calling Mr. Black
He would check on Jaliyah
I would feel better about that
After three hours I landed
And I couldn't believe this was happening
I left my damn phone
On the kitchen counter at the cabin
I took a taxi to my hotel
Since I couldn't use my app for Lyft
I had Jaliyah's and Malcolm's number memorized
I couldn't believe this shit
I called Jaliyah
It went straight to her voicemail
I called Malcolm
No answer. What the hell?

The Cabin

Jaliyah

<u>An unwelcomed surprise from a very creepy guy.</u>

I made it back to the cabin
The rain was about to pour
I had made it inside
And was about to close the door
That landscaper Mike popped up
That helped when I hurt my toe

He explained, "I'm so sorry to bother you
But my car broke down up the road
Can I use your phone?
My phone battery died."

I hesitated, "Sure just a minute."

He asked, "Mind if I wait inside?"

"Okay. It is about to storm."

He agreed, "Thanks it's getting chilly out
In here it's nice and warm."

I replied, "Thankfully
The heating system is finally repaired
We won't need to keep bringing
Fire logs here, there and everywhere."

I went in my purse
And passed him my phone
He questioned, "Where's Sebastian?
I can't believe he left you here alone."

"He'll be back soon."

I lied feeling a little uneasy

"I'm surprised he left you here
I sure wouldn't have, believe me."

I laughed a bit
I insisted, "Go ahead and make your call
Did you need a charger for your phone?"

He responded, "No not at all
I left it in my car
I took a chance on you being here
And look, here we are."

I sighed, "Yeah
That's crazy right."

He smiled, "Let me call this tow truck
Hopefully, they don't take all night."

Jayson

<u>Preparation is key, if the baby belongs to me.</u>

Charae called me back
She sounded a little sad
She said she got Jaliyah's email
And she understood her being mad
She told me she spoke with her doctor
About the issues with paternity
And that I needed to come to the next appointment
The test would determine who was the father
The other guy or me
I told her I would be there
Because I needed to know
That it would push my timeline up
If I had a baby, I needed to prepare for

She agreed, "You're right
I'm sorry we're in this position."

"Yeah, so am I
But I will handle my business."

LaRhonda N. Felton

Sebastian

<u>Coming, going and the uneasy feeling of not knowing.</u>

I tried Malcolm a second time
No answer again
Not making contact with anyone
Was becoming frustrating
I reached out to my ex mother-in-law
To let her know I was in town
She let me know she would send a car
I said I would be down
I couldn't shake this feeling
I was worried
But the car would be here any minute
I had to hurry
I used the hotel's guest computer
And paid triple to change my flight
Fuck leaving tomorrow
I'm flying back in tonight

Jaliyah

<u>You must take heed when your instincts scream.</u>

I walked into the kitchen
But I didn't too go far
I wanted to make sure
He called the tow truck to help with his car
And much to my surprise
I spotted Sebastian's phone
I put it in my pocket

He chuckled, "Oh now come on."

Damnit, I had no idea
He was standing behind me

"Sebastian left his phone
On the counter I see."

"Oh he did, did he?
Is that what you put in your pocket?"

I trembled, "Yes, I will put it up."

"No, you won't, now drop it
Sebastian thought he was doing something
Last week, treating me like shit
And you just sat there and watched it unfold
Didn't you, bitch?"

Before I could respond
He punched me so hard
I fell to the floor
All I saw were stars

"Say something now bitch!"
He repeatedly yelled
"You rich bitches

Can rot in hell
I lost my job
All because you stubbed a *toe*
I came back here today
To make you pay ho
Give me that fucking phone
Before I break your face
I have nothing left to lose
And today is the day you pay!"

After that he punched me again
I tried to turn over to get off my back
But he kept on punching me
Until everything went black

Sebastian

<u>Sad tears and mounting fears.</u>

I tried Mr. Black again
Once I got to the funeral home
This time he picked up
I explained Jaliyah was alone
I told him about Bianca
And the reason I had to leave
He confirmed he would check on Jaliyah
And extended his sympathies
I told him I was worried
That I'd even changed my flight
And I would be returning soon
Flying back in tonight
Malcolm promised Jaliyah would call
And leave a message at the hotel
I tried calling my own phone
It went straight to voicemail
After a couple hours Bianca's service was over
But it didn't seem quick enough
I raced back to the hotel
And grabbed my stuff
I checked for messages
At the front desk
The clerk assured me
There had been none left

I got a taxi
And headed straight to the airport
There was no need sitting in that room
What was I waiting around for?
I got to the airport
And it was three hours before my flight
I called Malcolm again
Even he had a feeling something wasn't right

He had gotten on the road
After he hung up with me
He called the sheriff in the area near the cabin
And he explained it was pouring
The sheriff also indicated that cell coverage was spotty
Which could explain not being able to get in touch
But that he would check out the cabin
Malcolm exclaimed, "Shit, he owes me that much!"

The Cabin

Jaliyah

<u>Black rain and excruciating pain.</u>

I woke up
In pain so intense
Why was he doing this to me?
It didn't make any sense
I told Sebastian that day
That he was only trying to help
Him getting fired
He couldn't blame on anyone else
He had me on the floor
Tied to a dining room chair
My face felt massive
And there was blood dripping from my hair
I could hear him in the background
Sounded like he was ransacking the place
He came back in again
All I remember was his boot coming towards my face

LaRhonda N. Felton

Sebastian

<u>Frantic hurry, constant worry.</u>

I would rather be safe than sorry
And do this all for nothing
I couldn't shake the nagging inside me
That it is truly something
I was pacing back and forth
They finally let me board the plane
The sickening feeling
Was driving me insane
Malcolm was picking me up
Since he was already making the drive
I was ready to be back on the ground
I couldn't wait to arrive

Jaliyah

<u>Paralyzing fear. Will I make it out of here?</u>

Oh my God!
My head hurt now more than ever
And the pounding seemed to be matching
The rhythm of the weather
I was still tied up
I kept going in and out
I couldn't tell if I was alone
Or if he was still in the house
The rain sounded so loud
But I couldn't really see
My eyes were so swollen
Everything appeared blurry
I thought I saw lights
Possibly from a car
But I couldn't make it out
Focusing was too hard
I closed my eyes
As the tears stung my face
Someone in the distance asked
"What the hell happened in this place?"

CHAPTER 13

LaRhonda N. Felton

Sebastian

<u>Unfair turn, fears confirmed.</u>

Another three hours
And I was back on the ground
Thankfully, air traffic let us land
The rain was really coming down
I raced out of the airport
Glad I only had a carryon
Malcolm was on the passenger side of the truck
I knew something was wrong
When I got to him

I questioned, "Is everything okay?
What happened to Jaliyah?"

I could see tears running down his face

"It's bad Sebastian,"
He managed to speak
"We need to head for the hospital
My baby's being taken there immediately."

I hit the steering wheel
I was mad as hell
I knew something was wrong
When I kept getting the voicemail

"What did the police say?
Did they tell you anything?"

"Only that the cabin has been torn apart
And she suffered one hell of a beating."

"Fuck!" I yelled
This was all too much
Bianca's suicide. Jaliyah assaulted
What the fuck?

The Cabin

When we got to the hospital
I damn near passed out
Jaliyah was unrecognizable
She had a bandage on her head and wires in her mouth
What the fuck happened?
Who the fuck had done this?
I was beyond angry
I was fucking livid
Malcolm was speechless
He could barely stand
I grabbed him by the shoulder
And he took my hand
I helped him to the chair
He was in an emotional hell
For the first time he appeared older
Weaker, almost frail

He pleaded, "Sebastian
Please call my wife
Tell Jacquelyn she needs to be
On the next flight."

He cried, "This is bad, this is very, very bad
I never expected her to be hurt like this
They need to find that son-of-a-bitch
The heatless bastard that did this shit."

I made the call to Mrs. Black
Her voice trembled with fright
Jacquelyn confirmed she would be
Landing later tonight
I used Malcolm's phone
And ordered her a Lyft
I went looking for the sheriff
Maybe he had some leads on this
He had gone back to the cabin
To gather evidence in the case
I went back to Jaliyah's room
My stomach churned every time I saw her face

LaRhonda N. Felton

They had her sedated
Awaiting the CT scan of her brain
She may need surgery
She may never be the same

A week went by
And Jaliyah was still asleep
I prayed she would wake up
Somehow return to me
There appeared some good news
Her CT was clear
The doctors were very concerned
Especially with blood coming from her ear
Her jaw was broken
Which was the reason for the wires
We were taking shifts at the hospital
But we were all extremely tired
I stopped by the cabin
And I just broke down and cried
The last place where we made love
Is the same place she almost died
There was blood everywhere
We were lucky she was even alive
I kept pondering to myself
How he even got inside
Was he lying in wait?
Was it someone she knew?
Police was going through the evidence
Hopefully, they had some concrete clues
But I needed to get back
My shift was up next
And I didn't plan on being late
Mr. Black needed to rest

Jayson

<u>Good news and bad. Things change so fast.</u>

I went to Charae's appointment
And the test was a breeze
They took blood from her
And the same amount from me
It took seventy-two long hours
And the results were in
I had a meeting with Charae
At her doctor's office again
We went in and sat down
To await our turn
Either way I was going to work after
I had money to earn
Charae looked tired
But I wasn't worried
I needed the doctor to come on
Because I was in a hurry
Today was a big day
I was moving into my own place
I had put my deposit down
They called us back, putting a smile on my face
Charae looked nervous
And understandably so
I took a seat in the office
Prepared for the blow
Whether or not
This baby was mine
I knew deep down
My life would be fine
The doctor looked at Charae
Then she looked at me

She confirmed, "Jayson, you aren't the father
I'm so sorry."

LaRhonda N. Felton

Charae broke down
That only meant one thing
That she would need to call
Dude from the restaurant again

I replied, "I'm sorry
I got the results I needed today
Thank you, Doc
See you later, Charae."

I left the doctor's office
With the greatest news
But then I saw a woman attacked at her family's cabin
Police searching for clues
I saw her name next
Jaliyah Black
I couldn't believe it
How had she been attacked?
I thought about it
All day at work
Who would do that?
She was too kind to hurt
When I got off
I mustered up the courage I had
And did what I knew I had to
I called Jaliyah's dad
I didn't think he would answer
But he sounded so full of despair
I knew it was serious if she was hospitalized
He agreed I could visit her there
He told me Jaliyah was in a coma
She had been beaten pretty bad
I informed him I would arrive the weekend
And hung up with her dad
I couldn't believe it
What a crazy ass day
I felt sorry for both
Jaliyah and Charae

LaRhonda N. Felton

Sebastian

<u>No news is good news, I guess.</u>
<u>This entire situation is a complete mess.</u>

I was barely sleeping
And when I did, I had nightmares
I felt so guilty for leaving Jaliyah
Without anyone else being there
Malcolm told me
If I apologized one more time
He would knock me out
We both ended up crying
But I was thankful
That her family knew
For Jaliyah
There wasn't anything I wouldn't do
Malcolm had hired a crew
For the cabin. Clean up and repairs
He confided he was contemplating
Putting the place up for sale
I honestly didn't think
That it was a bad idea
Because I knew Jaliyah would never go back
Once she got out of here
Malcolm told me
About Jayson's phone call
That he may come up
So, I would meet him after all
Jaliyah's swelling was
Dwindling slow
When she would wake up
They didn't know
The doctors advised
She would continue sleeping
The recovery process is tricky
Her body knew best what she needed

The Cabin

Malcolm got a call
From the foreman at the cabin
He advised we needed to come out
Good, I wanted to know what was happening

LaRhonda N. Felton

Jayson

<u>Change can be sweet, but I need her here with me.</u>

I moved into my new place
I was too damn excited
So far it was nice
The area seemed quiet
I rented a car for the weekend
And checked my hotel reservation
I was going to see Jaliyah
A far cry from a vacation
But I was glad to be able to show
I had made some progress
And even though we weren't together
I didn't love Jaliyah any less
She would always be special to me
More special than anyone else
She didn't deserve any of this
She deserved only the best

How could I have been so stupid?
I hope I have the opportunity
A chance to show Jaliyah
That she means the world to me
I don't care what it is
I'm willing to do whatever it takes
To make her love me again
And forgive my epic mistake

The Cabin

Sebastian

<u>A face from her past. Some questions answered at last.</u>

Jacquelyn stayed at the hospital
I told Malcolm to be prepared
The last time I was here
The place looked like hell
That coward didn't only beat Jaliyah
He had torn the place apart
I wanted to find him before the police
So, I could rip out his fucking heart
Punk motherfucker
I bet he won't fight a man
But if I find him first
I'm stomping his ass

We pulled up to the cabin
And the foreman met us in the driveway
He inquired, "Does this belong to either of you?
We stumbled upon it today."

I recognized that toolbox
From the day Jaliyah stubbed her toe
But Mike had taken it with him
He had it when he was let go

Malcolm answered, "No, I've never seen it before."

I lied, "No it's not mine
But I'll check with the landscaping crew
That was here the last time."

I put in an immediate call to the owner
Quietly, so that Malcolm wouldn't know
If that fucker Mike came back here
I would make him reap what he sowed

LaRhonda N. Felton

I got the owner's voicemail
I left a message, "Get back to me A.S.A.P
I need to know the whereabouts
Of your former employee."

I went back to the hotel
Mr. Black went to his room
I got showered and dressed
My shift at the hospital was coming up soon
I checked my phone
And noticed a missed call
It wasn't who I was expecting
But instead my ex mother-in-law
Her message was curt
But totally her attitude
I didn't call her back
I would check my voicemail in the hospital room
I grabbed my blanket
And a bag of chips
I needed to get a good run in tomorrow
My exercise had gone to shit
I grabbed the book
I read to Jaliyah at night
She hadn't woken up yet
But I was praying she might
I wanted to hold her, squeeze her
And kiss her face
The time would come soon
But for now, she needed space
To heal thoroughly
To feel like herself
But I promised with my life
She wouldn't be hurt by anyone else

I made it to the hospital
I told Mrs. Black it looked like rain
She cried, "Thank you for being here, Sebastian."

I hugged her, and promised, "I will call if there's any change."

I was in the room for a few hours
And there was a knock at the door
I responded, "Come in" and in walked a guy
I'd never seen before
Thinking to myself
This must be Jayson, the cheater

He seemed confused
"Jayson? I'm Sebastian. It's nice to meet you."
He confirmed, "Jayson Reyes."

I shook his hand

"I thought so
Thanks for coming man."

He gasped when he saw Jaliyah
He sighed, "Oh my God!"

I admitted, "She's looking more like herself
But seeing her this way has been hard
Pull up a chair
Sit for a while."

"Do they have any idea who did this?
He must've been out of his mind."

"No but when I catch him
He will be
I'm gonna leave him so close to death
His ass will be barely breathing."

Jayson remarked, "I agree
She didn't deserve this."
"Oh, I'm fucking him up on sight
Not on accident but on purpose."

He agreed, "I'm with you on that."

I replied, "Don't bullshit me man."

"I'm here until Tuesday
Let me know if and when you find his ass."

I nodded, "Bet it up
I'm waiting on the call now
But tell me, how did you mess up with Jaliyah?
What was that all about?"

Jayson looked weird
Then he took a seat
We had nothing but time
He explained the whole relationship to me

I finally checked my voicemail
My ex mother-in-law was livid
I called her back and bluntly asked her
"Delores, what is it?"

She yelled, "I don't know why my daughter loved you so much."

"What did I do now?"

"Just shut the fuck up!"

"Now wait a damn minute!"
I stepped out of the room
"You are way out of line or full of grief I assume
But I am a grown ass man
And you are testing my restraint
I want to cuss your ass out
But out of respect for Bianca, I can't
You keep on though
And I lay down the respect
And let your ass have it
Now what's next?"

The Cabin

She calmed down a bit
And replied, "Here's the deal
You are the sole beneficiary
In her will!"

"I never asked her to do that."

"Yeah well, she did
And it's something
I will never forgive
My husband's policies
Willed from Bianca to you
This is something
I never thought she'd do
I raised that girl right
But somehow you turned her head
And you were never satisfied
You were in so many women's beds
Living out your fantasies
Sowing your wild oats
You were never any damn good
Just a low-down nasty ho.
Her lawyer is sending an email
And documents for you to sign
Your trifling ass will then possess
Everything that should've been mine."

She hung up
With her filthy mouth
It was good she did
Before I cussed her out
It wasn't my fault
Delores was a hateful witch
Bianca did what she wanted
I never asked her for shit

CHAPTER 14

LaRhonda N. Felton

Jayson

<u>Black eyes and one hell of a surprise.</u>

Damn seeing Jaliyah
Made me feel so sad
I didn't expect this dude Sebastian
I just knew it would be her dad
Sebastian and Jaliyah
He seemed very close to her in a short span of time
But I can't blame anyone but myself
The fuckup was mine
It's wild though
She managed to stay asleep
When all these damn machines
Do is beep
I went closer to her
And held her hand

I whispered, "Jaliyah it's Jayson
Wake up if you can
There's a lot of us here
That need you alive
So, we can laugh at your corny jokes
And see that beautiful smile
I need your forgiveness
For my stupid mistakes
I hope we can be friends
If not now, then someday
I'm leaving for the night
But Sebastian will be here with you
Come on wake up beautiful
This is something you got to fight through."

Sebastian came back in
I could see the tears in his eyes
He stole the love of my life
I wanted to but couldn't really hate the guy

The Cabin

Jaliyah

<u>Noisy machines and three sets of eyes staring back at me.</u>

I thought I heard voices
They seemed so far away
My eyelids felt so heavy
I couldn't find the words to say
Then all of a sudden
It got so quiet
Except for this constant beep
That made me frightened
I wanted to wake up
But it seemed so hard
I don't want to be here
I want to go to the park
To go down the slide
My daddy pushing me on swings
And then we'd play hopscotch
And eat cold ice cream
I have ponytails
With bows
And mama is mad
Because I got ice cream on my clothes

She complained, "I always make a mess
And she is tired of me
Then daddy stated, "It's no big deal
just a little ice cream."

Now, I'm watching Soul Train
And Beverly Hills 90210
Why am I watching this?
These shows are so old
I see Charae sitting in my room
We are going to the Funk Fest
She needs to borrow my shoes
I wondered, "Damn what's next?"

LaRhonda N. Felton

I see Jayson
And now this new guy Sebastian
Now I see this man Mike
Inside our cabin
Oh no! He's mad
And he's mean
I can't get away
And I can't scream
I want to wake up
Someone calls my name
The man is hitting me
No! Not again
I hear someone yell

"Please come quick, she's waking up."

And a bright light in my eyes
It's all too much

I squint and blink
Trying to see
There are three sets of eyes
Staring back at me
My dad's, my mom's
And some stranger
She's my doctor I assume
Thank God I'm out of danger

Where is Sebastian?
Did he ever make it back?
I took him to the airport
She died. Bianca, his ex-wife
Things seem a little sketchy
How long have I been asleep?
I want to know what happened
Everyone is staring at me

I look at my dad
He has a face full of tears

My mom is crying too
Thank God I'm still here

The doctor spoke first "Welcome back
I'm going to check your vitals okay?
We're so glad you woke up
What a great way to start the day."

My mom and dad
Looked tired yet relieved
I want to ask, how long have I been here?
How long have I been asleep?

The doctor warned, "Don't try to speak
Your jaw has to mend
But we can still communicate
I have a tablet and a pen
You can also use your eyes
By blinking twice for yes and once for no
But we aren't going to bombard you
We will take things slow
If you get tired
Or you feel any stress
Close your eyes
And we will let you rest
Rest is a vital part of healing
And we will take it one day at a time
And we want a full recovery
You're awake now and that's a positive sign."

The doctor checked this
And checked that
Then she advised
"Now you can rest, Ms. Black."

My dad just held me
But he looked so tired
I wanted my parents to know I loved them
But my jaw was wired

LaRhonda N. Felton

I wrote it on my tablet
Which took more effort
But they both deserved to know
That to me they were special
Looking at my mom
I vowed to do better
I thanked God for keeping me here
So, we would have more time together
My dad told me
That Sebastian would be here soon
Much to my surprise
Him and Jayson both walked into my room

Jayson

Sunday morning and blessings dawning.

Sunday morning
And I woke up starving
I never expected to see
Sebastian in the hotel lobby
Turns out he had a room here too
It made sense with the hospital being close by
He could get there quickly
Morning, noon, or night

He admitted, "I'm glad I ran into you
Jaliyah is awake
Her dad just called
I'm heading that way."

I smiled, "That's amazing
I will be there soon
I left my car keys
Up in my room."

Sebastian suggested, "It's cool
Or if you have everything you need
I don't mind
You can ride with me."

I thought about it
And I had my wallet

"You know what
I will take you up on that offer."

We headed to the hospital
I couldn't tell which of us was more excited
The funny thing is
Neither one of us tried to hide it

Jaliyah looked shocked
When we both came in the door
But when we explained how it happened
She seemed to relax a bit more
I didn't think she would be happy
Especially seeing my face
But she knew why I was here
And she gave me a small embrace
Even her dad
Didn't seem so uptight
But considering the circumstances
We didn't need to fight
Jaliyah had obviously moved on
And that did hurt
But she deserves to be happy
No need for me to act like a jerk

Sebastian

<u>Thankful, blessed and alleviating stress.</u>

I couldn't have been happier
When Malcolm called
God had heard my prayers
And answered the most important one of all
I raced to get dressed
Showered and brushed my teeth
My stomach was growling now
Reminding me I didn't eat
I went to grab a sandwich
And a big bouquet of balloons
Just a little something
To decorate my baby's room
My phone was buzzing
Caller ID displayed Benton Landscaping
I knew immediately
This was a call I was taking

"Sebastian, I got your call
Seems you're looking for Mike?"

I confirmed, "Yes, I'm looking for his ass."

"Turns out, you aren't the only one.
I also got a call from his wife
He has a little spot he goes to
When he wants to get away
Small little fishing shack
Over off Homer and Bay
You know that area?"

"Not exactly, but I'll find it
I appreciate you calling me back."

He said, "I didn't mind a bit
But let me warn you Sebastian
He can be a little squirrelly when he's in the wrong
If you plan on going out there
I would suggest not going alone
I was hoping he wasn't that stupid
To go back and hurt Ms. Black
He deserves whatever he gets
To hurt a woman like that."

I stressed, "Oh and Benton
We never had this conversation."

"Sebastian, my friend,
That goes without saying."

I took the balloons
Back to Jaliyah's room
Switched shifts with Malcolm
So, he would be leaving soon
Malcolm looked suspicious

He whispered, "Is everything alright?"

"Yeah, just something came up
I need to deal with tonight."

Jayson looked at me
I needed to make sure he was still down to ride
I didn't care either way
I was seeing Mike's ass tonight

I caught the drop on the family
And pulled Jayson to the side

I confirmed, "I got that address
You still down to ride?"

"Oh absolutely
I just need to swing by the room
Put on some sweats
And change my shoes."

"Bet, I will be in the lobby tonight,
around ten."

He agreed, "I will be there too
See you then."

I went into Jaliyah's room
Jayson rode back with the Blacks
I wanted some time alone with her
We really needed that
I looked at Jaliyah

"Baby, I apologize
I should have never left you."

She had tears in her eyes

"I kept calling and calling
And getting voicemail
I felt something was wrong
Not being there was pure hell."

She motioned for her tablet and wanted to write

She wrote, *It wasn't your fault
You didn't know what would happen that night
Is he in jail?*

She was looking at me
"Not yet baby, but he will be
The cops are looking for him
And I've been in touch with his old boss
He's going to pay for what he did
He will be caught."

LaRhonda N. Felton

I kissed her and hugged her
Before she fell asleep
I couldn't wait until the day
She could fall asleep with me

It was five minutes to ten
And I headed to the lobby
If Jayson wasn't ready
I was leaving him
Sorry not sorry
I needed to handle this shit
Mike had been breathing easy far too long
I wasn't going to kill him
But I was planning to break a few bones
Jayson was waiting
In a pair of old Timbs
Funny thing is
I was dressed almost identical to him
Sweats, Timbs, and a hoody
Ass-kicking clothes
I will call the cops anonymously
Once old boy starts to doze
I got in the truck
With Jayson right next to me

I detailed, "We won't park at his spot
But on the next street
I asked, "Did you leave your phone?"

He answered, "Yes back in the room."

"Great minds think alike
I left mine too."

Jayson laughed and remarked,
"No face, no case."

I chuckled, "True and no phone
No trace

Jayson, look I don't want
You to feel obligated to do anything
I know you and Jaliyah broke up
You don't have to explain."

He acknowledged, "You're right
I fucked up in a major way
And I'm not pressed
But we're kicking his ass today."

With that being said
I picked up speed
Headed to get this fucker
And let the ass kicking proceed

Jayson

Keeping my word. It's the least she deserved.

Sebastian must've thought
I was blowing smoke
When I agreed I was down to ride
Absolutely not
Nope
I wanted old boy to pay
Whoever the fuck he is
So, on the ride over
I asked him what's the real
What made this man
Flip the fuck out
And what the hell
Made him come back to the house
Sebastian explained
The day Jaliyah stubbed her toe
And he checked dude
For his toolbox being left in the floor
He mentioned he came in the kitchen
And dude literally picked Jaliyah up
That the shit was highly inappropriate
I told him say no more
I'd heard enough
He was right
Dude overstepped
And we were kicking his ass
Close to his last breath
We decided on the ride over
What would be the best approach?
Getting in and getting out
This shit was no joke
Sebastian hit the lights
As he parked under a tree
There were no houses on this end
So, it would be difficult for anyone to see

We pulled the hoodies up
And snuck around the back
Old boy was watching TV
In this rundown ass shack
I knocked on the front door
While Sebastian waited on the side
Old boy had no idea
But he had fucked up this time

LaRhonda N. Felton

Sebastian

<u>Two pairs of Timbs and a few broken limbs.</u>

I was waiting on the side
When Jayson knocked on the door
As the door opened, he asked Jayson, "Who are you?"
Jayson knocked his ass on the floor

We both went inside
And snatched his ass up quick
When he saw me standing there
He yelled, "Oh shit!"

"Oh shit is right motherfucker."

He sneered, "I should've killed that bitch and left the door locked
I knew she would snitch."

"She didn't say shit bitch, you left your fucking toolbox."

I punched him in his face
No further words were exchanged
Between Jayson and I
We brought the pain
His eyes were closed
And he was missing some teeth
And now, his jaw was broken
Thanks to me

I put them Timbs
Right in his face
And we left his blood
All over his place
We hurried back to the truck
And drove a few miles up the road
I pulled over and got out the duffel bag
With a clean set of clothes

I took out the burner phone
And called the cops
I gave them the address
To old boy's spot
We went in the woods near the cabin
And put the duffel and the burner in a fire

I advised Jayson, "We will never speak of this night again."

He confessed, "We share the same desire
Jaliyah doesn't need to know."

"I feel the same way
I don't want what we did
Somehow impacting her case
I never thought our meeting
Would involve us keeping a secret."

Jayson replied, "Same here
But I know we will both keep it
You love Jaliyah, Sebastian
And that's what she needs
She deserves the best
And sadly, she didn't get that from me
Don't get me wrong
I still have love for her but I'm stepping aside
She asked me for space
And I need to oblige."

I looked at him
And confirmed, "We agree on that too
But I'm glad you had my back on this."

Jayson admitted, "It's what I needed to do."

CHAPTER 15

Jayson

Facing the truth… and the new guy too.

Sebastian drove us back to the hotel
He went to his room and I went to mine
I was leaving Tuesday morning
I would visit Jaliyah one more time
My life had changed
So much over the last few months
Some of it I liked
Some of it I didn't want
But choices had been made
With consequences that couldn't be undone
The fact that I lost Jaliyah
Was a life lesson and a painful one
If I'm being honest with myself
I'm more independent on my own
I don't have a safety net
I'm now my own backbone
Jaliyah and I
Had our time
And even though I wasn't ready
She was no longer mine
But I felt okay with the fact
She was in good hands
Even her daddy seemed to like
This dude named Sebastian

Sebastian

<u>Breaking news and feeling blue.</u>

Breaking news cut in
On the television screen
Police lights were flashing
They were live on the scene
An arrest had been made
In the case of Jaliyah Black
They had found the person responsible
For the cabin attack
It seemed he was beaten
By someone he wasn't identifying
And even when cops pressured him
He wasn't cooperating
And I knew why
Mike would be silent for life
If he cared anything about
His children and his wife
Truthfully, I wouldn't hurt them
But Mike didn't have a clue
He didn't know for certain
What I would or wouldn't do
I went back to the hospital
Malcolm looked me up and down

"Sebastian, did you see the news?
That asshole was found."

I replied with a happy grin,
"Yes, I saw it on the news
Seems someone whipped his ass."

Malcolm questioned, "You got any clues?"

I didn't say a word
Simply shook my head
I sat in the chair closest to Jaliyah's bed

Malcolm admitted, "I would love to know who it was
So, I can shake that man's hand
Because I know that bastard
Won't ever hurt my baby again."

I quipped, "Who knows
Maybe you'll get the chance someday."
Malcolm shook my hand
And smiled, "Let me get out of the way."

Once Malcolm left
An e-mail alert buzzed
With everything going on
I had no idea what it was
An e-mail from an attorney
Requesting a call back
And signatures needed
On the documents attached

The e-mail mentioned
A letter only to be opened by me
That he would need an address
To ensure its prompt delivery

The next morning
A courier at the hotel
Called for me to come down
I needed to sign for mail
I couldn't imagine what this was
That Bianca sent to me
Once I saw her handwriting
I knew I would need privacy

Sebastian my love
Where do I begin?
Hopefully, you understand
Why I needed this pain to end

The Cabin

The day we met
Was the happiest day of my life
Only surpassed by the day
You asked me to be your wife
I remember it so vividly
I had a flat and you stopped to help
You were so handsome
I was instantly beside myself
I couldn't even speak
When you questioned if I had a spare
I offered to pay you
But you wouldn't dare
Helping a beautiful woman in distress
You referred to it as your duty
I was still stuck on the fact
That looking at me, you saw beauty

I couldn't let our encounter end there
I offered to buy lunch
You said you'd go
But only if we went Dutch
I made the first move
And I felt like that was my downfall
I also asked for your number
And made the first call

We had chemistry
And I thought it would be enough
But it never was
At least not for us
We had a decent sex life
I can admit I was pleased
Which is why I was so shocked
To learn of your infidelities
I thought we got past it
Because things for us were good again
But in all actuality
You just became better at hiding them

LaRhonda N. Felton

I needed you for too much
Being your wife validated me
I was too naive to realize
That was too much responsibility
It wasn't your job
To fill my gaps
I was the only one
With the ability to change that

I never stopped loving you, Sebastian
Since the first day we met
And that love consumed me
I had nothing left for myself
I prepared for and planned
Our wedding day down to a T
Never once suspecting
You were nowhere near ready
You weren't a man yet
But my love remained
I thought if I just loved you enough
You would stop causing me pain

I read relationship books
I went to counseling and took classes too
It didn't matter what I did
None of it pleased you
We were married five years or more
Before it finally clicked
That you were the only one
Not growing or changing while in it
I tried cheating back
Something you never knew
But not even another man
Could lessen my love for you
My mother thought I was a fool
And for the most part she was right
But it wasn't her marriage
And I felt we deserved the fight
The first time I filed for divorce

The Cabin

It ripped my heart out
And I was filled with anxiety
And tremendous doubt
I had you served on your job
To scare some sense into you
It was the most terrifying
Thing I'd ever had to do

You came to me
And begged for another chance
Convincing me somehow
That you were a changed man
And for the first time in years
I saw us with a future
But it was short-lived
You went right back to what you were used to
All those different women
And the blatant disrespect
I really didn't know
What to expect next
There was no changing my mind
The last time I filed
I wasn't fighting for me
I fought for our unborn child
I'm sorry I never told you
I needed you to fight for me
Not just exist in our marriage
And not because of a baby

As you may have guessed by now
Our baby didn't survive
I miscarried at nine weeks
My mom was there the entire time
I loved you then
And sadly, I love you now
I hope you find it in your heart
To forgive me somehow
When you finally reached out
To apologize to me

LaRhonda N. Felton

I wanted to tell you then
But I decided to just let it be
You see for most of our marriage
I blamed myself
That you always seemed happier
With someone else
When you came to my dad's funeral
I fantasized about the chance
A possibility of rekindling
Our long-lost romance
But you were different
And you weren't checking for me
It was like losing you a second time
Along with my daddy
So, you see, the two men I loved the most
Were gone, never to return
And this all has been so unbearable
I don't want to continue to yearn
For a love from you
That you don't feel for me
And it hurts too bad
To continue suffering

I want the pain to end
And I'm tired of being alone
I've thought everything through
And this pain will end once I'm gone
Don't think this is your fault
Or that you may have changed my mind
You're great at a lot of things Sebastian
But not even you can stop me this time
This may surprise you
But I pray you find the love of your life
Be a good man for her
Settle down and make her your wife

And even if you never marry again
Be good to yourself

The Cabin

This letter and a few other things
Will be all that's left

One more thing
Take it easy on my mom
She barks viciously
But she really means no harm
Don't be surprised
I'm leaving everything to you
Everything my dad willed to me
And our old house too
I thought of changing my will
But I never did
I feel okay with that
Because in the end we were friends
I knew that you'd changed
And for the better this time
You were there when I needed you
You gave me peace of mind

My arrangements have been made
I didn't want arguing over that task
Once my body is found
Things should progress fast
I'm feeling drowsy now
I guess the pills are kicking in
I love you still
My beautiful, beautiful Sebastian

"Damn Bianca!"

This letter made me feel like shit
Even with all the apologies
It shouldn't have ended like this
She deserved better
So much better than me
Delores had a right to be angry
Bianca left me everything

LaRhonda N. Felton

From this day forward
I made a new vow
To make it up to her
Some way, some how

A few more weeks had passed
And tomorrow Jaliyah was being released
None of us had gone back to the cabin
And instead rented an Airbnb
Dealing with this situation
Jaliyah's family and I had become so close
And we were rallying around her
Which is what she needed most
Her jaw was healing nicely
And the wires were being removed next week
She still had a long road ahead of her
But I would be happy to hear my baby speak
Jayson had called Malcolm
A few times just to check in
And it was crazy to think
We could actually be friends
He was doing well for himself
And he loved that new job
But I didn't push a friendship
For Jaliyah it might be a little hard
As for Mike
His arraignment went well
He was kept in the county lock up
And given no bail
He was charged with
Attempted murder in the first degree
And that was due to his pre-meditation
And the extent of Jaliyah's injuries

Jaliyah

Finally being released. Trying to get back on my feet.

I'm so excited
I am being released
And then these wires
Come off next week
Sebastian has been amazing
My entire family has given me strength
I know I wouldn't have come through this
Had it not been for them
I'm so thankful to be alive
So many things I want to accomplish
Some things I need to work on
If I'm really being honest
For the moment
My focus is on healing
And making sure
I'm in touch with my feelings
I've had some very angry days
That I've swallowed and suppressed
Using the fact that I can't speak
As the reason I haven't confessed
But I know I need to work on me
Tackle this emotional hell
Maybe if Mike was dead
All would be well

LaRhonda N. Felton

Jayson

<u>Doctor's, neighbors and party favors.</u>

I had accomplished a lot
In a small amount of time
I'm loving my job
And this apartment of mine
I spoke with Malcolm the other day
And I couldn't believe he invited me
They're having a celebration for Jaliyah
And I'm attending the festivities
I talked to Charae last week
And she's been laying low at home
Turns out the father cut her off
So, she will raise her baby alone
She mentioned her neighbor
Being nice to her and keeping an eye out
I laughed and asked her was she talking about dude
With the cameras surrounding his house
She admitted yes that he was a doctor
And he was making sure she was okay
Bringing her food
And checking in every other day

I told her about Jaliyah
And I could tell she got upset
She couldn't believe what happened
And that she had so many regrets
I told her I did too
But I had to let that go
I was learning from my mistakes
And continuing to grow
I told her that I would check on her
When I got back in town
I didn't tell her where I was going
That the Black's invited me to come around

I didn't want to hurt her
Or make her feel more ostracized
We made a little small talk
And ended with goodbyes
I was heading out anyway
I was going on a date
With a girl I met at work
And I wasn't going to be late

CHAPTER 16

LaRhonda N. Felton

Jaliyah

<u>Healing takes time, but it begins in your mind.</u>

I was hospitalized
For five weeks
Certain nurses became friends
They took amazing care of me

Sebastian picked me up
And I was glad to leave
But I will admit
I had some anxiety
Going home or something like it
To the Airbnb
I wasn't sure how to feel
Or what was expected of me
Once inside the truck
And Sebastian began driving away
Tears fell from my eyes
Because I didn't feel safe
He looked over at me
And he held my hand
And even though I couldn't talk
He seemed to understand

He reassured me,
"Baby, it's okay. Cry if you need to
But I will lay down my life
Before anything else happens to you
"I love you, Jaliyah."
And even though I couldn't say it back
It was all over my body
And I know he felt that

Being home a couple of days
Had given me a little relief
But I would be lying
If I denied I didn't still feel the anxiety

Especially at night
Or like yesterday when it rained
I felt like I was alone with Mike
In that cabin again
My dad turned on some music
To try and lighten the mood
I ended up in the bed
I felt safer in my room
Sebastian came in
And held me until I fell asleep
And when I woke up this morning
He was still holding me
I wanted to ask about his therapist
To see if she had any openings
I felt like I was slipping away
I wanted to be seen soon, at least I was hoping

Sebastian

**<u>Physical bruising disappears.
But inside, trauma is a flame reignited by fear.</u>**

Watching Jaliyah shake in fear
Pissed me off in a major way
Mike got three hots and a cot
And she isn't living normally day to day
She was constantly watching the door
Always on high alert
And when it rained
She damn near jumped out of her shirt
I keep an eye on her
Reassuring her I'm here
And I'm not leaving her side
I hope that's clear
She's trying to be strong
But she doesn't need to be
We're all here for her
Loving her unconditionally

Jaliyah

<u>Sunny days keep most triggers away.</u>

The past couple of days
Things felt a little better
Although the memories of that day
Were triggered by rainy weather
My dad decided to put the cabin up for sale
And that broke my heart
I know how much he loved the place
The peaceful isolation was his favorite part
He said the isolation
Didn't keep me safe
It gave that man the freedom
To almost take me away
And losing me
Was more than he could bear
He knew after what happened
I could never return there
I told him I might
For him I would try
The conversation was too much
Because we both broke down and cried
My dad held me so long
With his nose in my hair
I didn't realize until then
How much I really needed him right here
I was immensely blessed
To still be alive
And so much more so
With the people I love by my side

I woke up this morning
Happy and excited
The wires are coming off today
And I couldn't be more delighted

I will have rubber bands in my mouth next
To continue the healing
And I'm fine with that
Being able to talk again is a great feeling
And to be honest feeling great lately
Has been few and far between
I don't want to trouble anyone
Because I know it's just me
My dad, Sebastian and even my mom
Have done everything they can
But my emotional health is off
Or not as stable as it was in the past
Sebastian has reached out to his therapist
And she is available tonight
I am going to do whatever it takes
To get back to my normal life
Sebastian came in the door
Looking fine and face fully bearded
I loved how he looked
And the texture was a smooth feeling
He kissed my face
And his smell intoxicated me
If it wasn't for my appointment
I would try lovemaking
Even though he's not having it
He wants me fully healed
But he smells so damn good
And Ms. Kitty is craving a feel

Sebastian

<u>Coming out of her shell… She's in there, I can tell.</u>

Jaliyah's energy felt different this morning
Almost like her old self
I was happy her parents were here
I also craved some time away from everyone else
I'm glad she has her appointment today
To remove the wires
I plan to cook for her soon
Whatever her heart desires
My parents fly in Thursday
And the party is set
With her wires being removed
This might be Jaliyah's best week yet

LaRhonda N. Felton

Jaliyah

<u>Wires removed, ready for some good food.</u>

The wire removal was a pain
Tomorrow I go to the dentist
With the healing that needs to be done
This whole process seems endless

Sebastian was driving
And yet he held my hand
It was crazy to me
How fast I fell in love with this man
I could barely speak
But he needed to know

I confessed, "Sebastian baby
I love you so."

He looked at me
"I love you too baby,"
With an intensity I've never experienced
"There are no ifs ands or maybes."

We drove the rest of the way in silence
Both of us loving being together
I was anxious about tonight's appointment
But I couldn't allow this anxiety to linger forever
I was now able to talk
Which meant I was also ready to eat

I turned and begged,
"Sebastian, when are you going to cook for me?"
He started laughing
I did too, even in pain

He said, "Soon enough
I'll be throwing down again."

Jayson

<u>New mates and amazing dates.</u>

My date with Sasha was awesome
And now I'm preparing for this weekend trip
But her and I have talked on the phone
Every night since
I thought of asking Malcolm
If I could bring her along
But I thought better of it
I figured it was best if I went alone
Give Jaliyah some time
And some added respect
I think my coming alone
Right now is for the best

I barely got an invite
So, I didn't want to rock the boat
I wanted things to be good between us
And they still are, I hope
Before I left the last time
Jaliyah let me know she was glad I came
I told her I appreciated being welcomed
And that even though things wouldn't be the same
I respect her
And I wanted her in my life
Even if it was as my friend
And not my wife
We communicated
Until she got tired of writing
And I was grateful for the chance
To talk without us fighting
Jaliyah was an amazing woman
And I lost her being dumb
But couch surfing taught me a lesson
And a very valuable one

Don't take someone's kindness for weakness
Thinking they won't ever leave
Because one day they will
And you will be sorry
I've learned a lot
Over the last few months
And I learned most
Not to rely on others so much
I can kind of see now
What Malcolm meant
When he told me I wasn't ready
But I was on the defense
Ready to show him how wrong he was
That he had no clue
Breaking his daughter's heart
Was something I would never do
He was right and I did
Broke her heart in the worst way
And I have regretted it ever since
In fact, every single day
Jaliyah will always
Have a special place in my heart
But I know I fucked up
And she deserves a fresh start
I checked my duffel
Making sure I had what I would need
Looking forward to the trip
Because this time it was for a party

Sebastian

<u>Party provisions and important decisions.</u>

Preparations were underway
And Malcolm seemed a little sad
Selling the cabin was his idea
I didn't think he would take it this bad
He was sitting on the porch
Of the rented Airbnb

I asked, "What's on your mind?
You know you can always talk to me."

He replied, "Everything and nothing
All at the same time."

I acknowledged, "More something than nothing
Seems to be running through your mind
Is it the cabin?
Are you upset about the sale?"

"Absolutely not", he answered
"For my baby that place represents hell
Besides, I'm making a nice profit
The buyer has wanted it a long time
And when I made him the offer
It almost blew his mind
The sale will be quick
No haggling or back and forth
And getting rid of it
Is what I want most
I am wondering though
We have this place for another few weeks
And I'm hoping that Jaliyah will consider
Coming home with me
At least for a little while
Until she's back on her feet."

LaRhonda N. Felton

I was a little taken aback

"I guess we'll see
The decision is up to her
And either way I won't interfere."

I didn't say what I was really thinking
Not now, not here
I had other ideas
But I wanted Jaliyah with me
Or wherever she went
Is where I wanted to be
I was putting plans in motion
To purchase or build a house
With my savings and inheritance
I could build one flat out
A conversation needed to be had
And Jaliyah had decisions to make
I wasn't going to pressure her
I wouldn't make that mistake
But I would let her know my plans
That I wanted her permanently in my life
And that when she's ready
To marry me and become my wife

I knew we were all tired
And could use a break
But we also wanted to be sure
The sentencing was over before leaving the state
Mike plead guilty
Sparing us the emotions of a trial
He would be sentenced next week
We wouldn't have to think about his ass for a while
I checked in with my parents
And made sure they were ready
I was excited about the party
Because the atmosphere felts so heavy
Maybe since talking with Malcolm
I was a little on edge

I didn't know what Jaliyah wanted
And I needed to get out of my own head
I wasn't going to dwell on the negative
And let it ruin our plans
I was going to talk to Jaliyah
I knew she would understand

CHAPTER 17

LaRhonda N. Felton

Jaliyah

<u>Questions and suggestions.
Going home felt like regression.</u>

The therapy session
Went well, at least I think it did
PTSD is most likely my issue
And maybe the case for years
Sebastian seemed worried
At dinner he didn't say much
I didn't question it at the time
I didn't want to make a fuss
He knocked on my door

"Baby, are you awake?"

I replied, "Sure, come in
I was just thinking about you anyway."

He asked, "Oh yeah?
What's on your mind?"

"You were quiet at dinner
Like you were in another space and time."

He sighed, "I'm sorry babe
I didn't mean to be distant."

"Talk to me."
I was being persistent

"Well your dad has his hopes up
That you would come home in a few weeks
And live with them
Until you're back on your feet."

"Oh? I had no idea he was making that assumption
And I'm not sure it will help
I need to rebuild my independence
Get back to depending on myself
I thank you all for being here
Because I need you
But at the same time
I need to get back to what I'm used to
And that's relying on me
Taking care of myself
Getting past my fear
And not being dependent upon anyone else."

He sighed, "Oh okay
What exactly does that mean?
Are you saying we have no future?
Elaborate and enlighten me please."

"Wait", I clarified, "That's not it at all
I want to be with you and share a life
But I also need my independence too
To feel whole again
And not like I'm helpless
I hope this is coming out right
And not sounding selfish."

He inquired, "So Jaliyah
What does us being together look like to you?
I don't want you to feel pressured
That's the last thing I'd do
But I do want to be sure
We're at least on the same page
And addressing what's necessary
You know what I'm saying?"

"Sebastian, I do
But I don't want to move too fast
I did the same thing with Jayson
And we both know that didn't last."

LaRhonda N. Felton

He shrugged, "You're right
Take the time you need
Let me know what you decide
I don't want you stressed about anything."

He kissed my forehead
And left the room
Leaving an energy behind
That felt like gloom

Sebastian

<u>Plans made, love delayed?</u>

What had happened here?
Had I read the signs wrong?
I thought Jaliyah and I were vibing
Seems we're not even singing the same song
I'm not giving up
But I do feel a little defeated
I thought us building a life together
Was what she wanted and needed
And her bringing Jayson up
Stung a little bit
I'm nothing like him
And I thought I had proven it
I won't jump to conclusions
I will let it play out
In the meantime, I will continue
My plans to move south

LaRhonda N. Felton

Jaliyah

Preparing myself, to avoid being victim to anyone else.

I wasn't sure what I wanted
Or where I wanted to go
I was convinced I wasn't going home
Why didn't I let Sebastian know?
I could tell he seemed surprised
And then looking at him
I recognized the hurt in his eyes
But I don't want to live together
Being another man's playmate
I wanted stability and commitment
Live-in girlfriend will not be my fate
Maybe it's too much too soon
Physically I was fine
But thoughts of hate
Consumed my mind
I wished Mike was dead
Every single day
And I would repent
Get on my knees and pray
Asking God for forgiveness
But then feeling like I lied
Because I'm not sorry for my thoughts
And I know I can't hide
I hate Mike for what he did
And the fact I didn't see
He had the advantage since I was alone
To take his anger out on me
I will do better
Learn to protect myself
I need self-defense classes
So I won't fall victim to anyone else

The Cabin

Jayson

<u>I learned quickly, I can depend on me.</u>

I got in my new truck
And hit the road
I was so proud of myself
Truth be told
In less than a year
I had a job and an apartment
An independent grown man
I love this feeling of contentment
Jaliyah leaving
Was the kick that I needed
To learn to do better
And I've succeeded
I talked to Charae
And her mom had moved in
To be there for her when the baby came
And her neighbor was still helping
Seems he had no family
And was glad to be of use
She said he dotes on her
And taking care of her is what he loves to do
I told her I was happy for her
Even though we were wrong
I wasn't going to dwell on it
I had been guilty for too long
Jaliyah had forgiven me
And that made Charae sad
Because I had been given that pardon
And she hadn't been given the same chance
I didn't make her any promises
But I would see how Jaliyah felt
And maybe she might email her
But not to hold her breath
She said that she wouldn't
She couldn't dwell on it either

That she had to focus on herself
And what her unborn child needed
I understood that
And told her I would check in when I got back
She begged me to tell Jaliyah
She was sorry to hear of her attack
And I may bring it up
Depending on the situation
I didn't want to cause
Any unnecessary agitation
I arrived at the hotel
And checked into my room
I grabbed a small snack
Since it would be dinnertime soon

The Cabin

Jaliyah

<u>Some sad situations facilitate much-needed rehabilitations.</u>

My mom knocked on the door
"Jaliyah? Sunshine, you asleep?

I answered, "No come on in."
She entreated, "Can you spare a little time for me?"
"Sure, Mom
What's going on?"

"I just wanted some time with you
Just us girls alone."

I sat down on the bed
"Okay that's fine
We haven't had much of that
What's on your mind?"

My mom smiled and confessed
"Actually, I did
I talked a lot while you were in the hospital
More than I have in years
Our relationship
Has always had a strain
And I know a lot of it is on me
And an image I wanted to maintain
I begged for your forgiveness
But you couldn't reply
I want us to be closer."

Then she started to cry
What in the hell? My mom, crying?
This is all too new
And so unexpected
It's not what I'm used to

I slid closer to hug her
"Mom, don't cry"
She lamented, "You have no idea
How afraid I was you might die
And the thought of how long we'd go
Without speaking or conversing
Had me regretful and on edge
Frightened and worried
We are better than that
And it's time to make amends
To get a relationship not only as mother and daughter
But to actually become friends
I admire your strength, Jaliyah
And how you go after what you want
In fact, I've been a little jealous
I can't even front."

I burst out laughing
Which hurt like hell
My mom using a word like *front*
I laughed so hard I almost fell

My mom looked up
And questioned, "What are you laughing at?"

"Mom, you used the word *front*
And I've never heard you speak like that."

My mom chuckled
"I'm hip, down with the times."
I screamed laughing
Tears falling this time

She said, "Come on now, Jaliyah
I'm trying to apologize."

I tried to calm down
And wiped my eyes

I confessed, "Mom listen
I've always wanted your love and respect
I just never felt I measured up
Or at least not yet
I felt you always scrutinized my choices
And disliked my ideas
Daddy has always had my back
And eased my fears."

She admitted, "I know honey
Please forgive my critical ways
I realize now how my behavior
Has kept you at bay
I want to change that
I know I can't erase the past
But we have time to make new memories
Happier ones that will last."

I looked at my mom
And I could see she was sincere
And I felt hope return
Removing all doubt and fear
We embraced each other tightly
And cried for what felt like weeks
I put my head in my mom's lap
And eventually asleep

LaRhonda N. Felton

Sebastian

<u>Hotel reservations and unexpected conversation.</u>

As I dropped my parents off at the hotel
I stopped by the bar for a drink
I really needed to make some sense of things
To be alone and think
I heard a voice from behind

"Hey man, are you still living here?"

I turned and saw Jayson
Sitting in a booth with a beer
I got my drink and went to his table
I answered, "No, but we're not far
I just helped my parents settle in
And came down to the bar."

"You look troubled
Is everything okay?"

I sighed, "Yeah, I'm maintaining
You know life and it's day-to-day."

Jayson inquired, "Jaliyah good?"

"Yeah, she is on the mend
And the party is coming together nicely
It's cool that you could make it back again."

Jayson looked at me and probed,
"Are you sure?
About the party I mean
I came back for the turn-up
But you don't look too festive to me."

I chuckled at the thought

I replied, "Just have a lot on my mind."

Jayson grimaced, "Let me guess
Mr. Malcolm Black this time?
Look, Sebastian, I've been there
And you and I aren't the same
But when it comes to his daughter
He is one stubborn ass man
And rightfully so
Jaliyah is a prize
But he can be a bit too possessive
At least he was in my eyes."

I heard Jayson's implication
And what he didn't voice as well
I hope he didn't think he had a shot at Jaliyah
There wasn't a chance in hell
Maybe my energy shifted
Or he saw the expression on my face

Because he pleaded, "Sebastian hear me out
Don't think I'm trying to make a play
I know for her and I, that ship has sailed
And from that guilt I'm finally free
I'm living my life
And working on being a better me
But as far as Mr. Black
Let Jaliyah work that out
She brings out his softer side
At least she did when I was around."

I debated, "I don't know about leaving it to her
I've always been able talk to him about anything."

Jayson replied, "Okay my brother
Don't forget my warning."

Jayson

<u>Conversations and beer with a man consumed with fear.</u>

Drinking my beer and waiting for dinner
I saw Sebastian come in
Dude looked sad
Like his world was ending
After talking with him
I knew it had to be Mr. Black
I remember the days
When I used to look like that
Down in the dumps
Like I would never measure up
Wondering if my love for Jaliyah
Would ever be enough
But I got over it
And ignored his ass
It put a strain on me and Jaliyah
Because I didn't get along with her dad
Sebastian finished his drink, got up and left
Said he had some last-minute details
I had a quiet dinner to myself
I called Sasha
And planned a date
Told her I wanted to see her when I got home
Hell, I had no reason to wait

CHAPTER 18

Sebastian

<u>Late night ride, she finally decides.</u>

"Zoom" by the Commodores
Blasted through the speakers giving me relief
The song calmed me before
Seeing Malcolm to make my speech
I planned to talk to Jaliyah
And her mother too
After I finished
She could decide what she wanted to do
But I couldn't accept Jayson's advice
And simply let things go
I wasn't built like that
And I needed everyone to know
I love Jaliyah
And our time together hadn't been long
But I was prepared to stick around
I was tired of being alone
I pulled up to the house
And Jaliyah came outside

She smiled, "Just the person I needed to see
Take me for a ride."

I agreed, "Okay."
I turned the ignition
The radio continued my playlist
Of easy listening

She stated, "I made up my mind
I want to be with you, but I don't want to play house
It's just not in me to do."

"Jaliyah, listen to me
I want you in my life
And not just to play house
I want you to be my wife."

"Sebastian, are you sure?
I mean marriage is a big step."

"You aren't feeling it?"
I thought to myself *What's next?*

"No, it's not that I don't feel it
It's just a whirlwind romance
With a traumatic event on the foothills
Do we even have a fair chance?"

"We have whatever we make it, Jaliyah
We have the right connection
If you want me, I'm yours
Through love, life and all the lessons."

She slid closer to me
She replied, "I'm in
I love you and want a life with you
I will marry you Sebastian."

"We must do this the right way
Let me talk to your dad
The last thing I want is for him to feel disrespected
And end up mad."

She agreed, "Oh of course
You handle it the right way
But we're getting married at the end of the day."

She laughed heartily
Her energy was much lighter
I was smiling from ear to ear
Glad I decided to wife her

I planned to get up early in the morning
Make it truly official and pick out her ring
I'd give it to her at the party
This news was worth celebrating

LaRhonda N. Felton

Jaliyah

**<u>Something old, something new.
Something borrowed and something blue.</u>**

I'm getting married
I was singing a song in my head
Sebastian was driving
And I couldn't wait for us to wed
Our relationship progressed quickly
On the backend of a bad break up
But I was pleased with our willingness to talk
And not ignore the big stuff
Sebastian makes me feel safe
And I see the love in his eyes
I feel it when he kisses me
This new love is a welcome surprise
I thought I wanted space
And to be left alone
But what I really wanted to find
Was someone to prove me wrong
That a real man does exist
And loves me just as much as my dad
A man willing to be honest with me
About everything in his past
I'm glad I didn't leave the cabin the first night
And gave Sebastian a chance
He was fine as hell from first sight
And now he's my man

The Cabin

Sebastian

<u>When it's right, be willing to fight.</u>

As we pulled up
Jaliyah's parents were sitting outside
I told Jaliyah, "I'm talking to him now."

I was nervous I can't lie
"Good evening
Mr. Black, can we talk?"

He asked, "Oh we're being formal now?
Sure, let's take a walk
It's a nice night
And I could use the exercise."

I saw Jaliyah take her father's seat
With a sparkle in her eyes
Once we were out of earshot
I got straight to the point

"I'm asking for your blessing
Because marrying Jaliyah is what I want."

He stopped dead in his tracks
And looked me in my eyes
He asked, "Are you sure?
Better yet, tell me why
You two barely know each other
What makes you think this will work?
Because I will not stand for
My daughter getting hurt
Don't get me wrong Sebastian
You're a good man
But still a work in progress
Why should I give you my daughter's hand?"

"Because I love her
And I need her in my life
She deserves a title
And that title is my wife
I know this is sudden
And it's taken you by surprise
But I'm willing to fight for her hand
I'm not accepting no, not this time."

Malcolm turned and questioned, "Is that right?
You're willing to defy me if I say no?"

"If that's what it takes sir
Jaliyah's worth fighting for."

Malcolm smiled and admitted
"That's what I needed to hear
Welcome to the family son!"
I needed to be sure
I'm putting my baby in good hands
Someone I can trust with her life
And you've proven that Sebastian
I know you kicked Mike's ass
I wish I had known
I would've loved to have gone with you
Left him with a few more broken bones."

We laughed and talked
As we headed back
Jaliyah and Jacquelyn were still on the porch

I declared, "Get ready to change your last name Ms. Black"

I went to bed late
But I didn't really sleep
I kept looking at ring styles
Since I was given Malcom's blessing
Emerald cut two carats
With baguettes on the side

Something that would sparkle
That matched Jaliyah's eyes
I got up early
And headed to the mall
I wanted the ring for the party tonight
I didn't have time to stall
I made my selection at the jewelry store
And didn't flinch at the price
The jeweler would have it ready by five
I was proud of myself, that ring was nice
I made it to the hotel
And the decorations looked amazing
It was a small event
That had become an even more special occasion
Our parents, a few friends
And some hospital staff
A thank you and welcome home for Jaliyah
We'd survived the aftermath

LaRhonda N. Felton

Jaliyah

<u>Forgiveness is key. I'm starting with me.</u>

What a beautiful morning
I felt better than I had in a long time
Visions of what I wanted for my wedding
Kept playing over in my mind
And then it hit me
I wouldn't have Charae
I'd always thought she'd be beside me
On my wedding day
My life had changed drastically
With losses and gains
With amazing amounts of happiness
Bringing rainbows after the rain
I sat on the side of the bed
And took a few deep breaths
I thanked God for my life
He had saved me from death
I realized just then
That I was meant to be here
And I became so full
I couldn't stop the flow of tears
My life meant something
And God wasn't done
I just kept saying thank you
He had brought me through the storm
Then something spoke to me
Saying you know what you must do
Forgiveness isn't for the perpetrators
Forgiveness blesses you
I picked up my phone
And dialed Charae

She answered, "Hello."

And through tears I whispered, "Hey."

She said, "Hi, Jaliyah
I never thought the day would come."

"To be honest me either
But this is something that needs to be done
You hurt me, Charae
You were my sister and you betrayed my trust
But let me make my point
I didn't call to fuss
I forgive you
You've always wanted everything I had
I just never ever thought
It would *ever* be my man."

"Jaliyah, wait
You're right and I will forever be sorry
I owe you so much
But I will begin with an apology
I thought I didn't need you
And behaved like I didn't care
I've been so selfish
You have always been there
Anytime I needed you
And God knows I require a lot
But this entire time
I never once stopped
To think of the hurt and pain
My behavior inflicted
I'm so glad Jayson asked you to call
And I am so grateful for your forgiveness."

"Jayson? Not at all
I haven't spoken to him."

"Then it's even more genuine
For you to call on a whim."

"Charae, after what I've been through
Forgiveness is key
And I'm not forgiving you for you
I'm forgiving you for me
I have been blessed
With a second chance at life
I have a man that loves and adores me
There isn't room in my heart for strife
With that being said
I wish you all the best
Congratulations on the baby
May you both be blessed."

"Thank you, Jaliyah,
I don't know what to say."

"It's okay, I need to get dressed
Enjoy the rest of your day."

I still had too much to do
When I ended the call
A party was being thrown for me
after all

Jayson

<u>Good news never comes too soon.</u>

As I was getting my clothes together
For the party tonight
Charae was calling my phone

I answered, "Is everything alright?"

She responded, "Thank you Jayson."

I was shocked, "Thanks for what?"

She cried, "For talking to Jaliyah
We just hung up."

I confessed, "Wow really?
It had nothing to do with me
I haven't talked to her yet
I was planning to at the party."

"She told me she forgave me
And she wished me well
The last time I saw her
She practically banished me to hell
I thought for sure
She had spoken with you
Either way, I'm so thankful
That she has forgiven me too."

"I'm happy you two talked
I know that eased your mind."

"Yes, it did. I apologized to her Jayson
And I really meant it this time."

LaRhonda N. Felton

We talked a little longer
And agreed to speak again soon
Things were better all around
This news made my afternoon

CHAPTER 19

LaRhonda N. Felton

Sebastian

<u>A beautiful surprise for the love of my life.</u>

I picked up the ring
And I was impressed
Jaliyah would love it
Now back to the hotel to get dressed
I got a room for tonight
Since I planned the party
I'm working smarter not harder
Less stress on me
I let my mom and dad know
That I had proposed
I was giving her the ring tonight
And that Jaliyah didn't know
My parents were excited
And very happy for me
My dad said with the growth I've made
I couldn't be more deserving
I was grateful
Because I had come a long way
I used to be a hot ass mess
Back in the day
Women would rush
Just to be around me
And working in corporate America
I gave them something to see
They used to think
They could sex me into commitment
Hell, I was already in a marriage
And not committed to it
I used to think we can have fun
For a few weeks at best
But don't get it twisted
I'm only committed to myself
I loved Bianca
But not the way she deserved

And when she decided she was leaving
I didn't think she had the nerve
Oh, I was full of myself
No humility or shame
Sexual satisfaction was
The game I was playing
But that wasn't me anymore
I turned in my player card
And I found loving one woman the right way
Wasn't all that hard
It was easy
And it felt right
I just knew Jaliyah
Was the love of my life

LaRhonda N. Felton

Jaliyah

<u>Life brings change, but family remains.</u>

My mom came in my room
And helped me get dressed
She chuckled, "I haven't done this in so long
I feel so blessed."

I confessed, "I'm glad mom
And so am I
But I need to ask you something
And try not to cry
I don't want you to ruin your make up
But here goes
Will you be my matron of honor?"

My mom's jaw hit the floor
She looked at me
With her eyes full of tears

"Are you serious, Jaliyah?
I never thought in a million years
That you would want me
Standing with you
But my answer is yes
There's nothing more I'd rather do."

We hugged each other
I heard my dad ask, "Well do wonders ever cease?
I can't believe it
Are my eyes deceiving me?"
I answered, "No, Daddy
Mom and I have made our peace."

"Yes, Malcolm
Our daughter has forgiven me."

The Cabin

He whispered, "This is magnificent
Tonight, will truly be a celebration
That's if you two will ever be ready
"Say no more", I ended our conversation

The decorations were spectacular
Sebastian had worked so hard
I couldn't believe my eyes
What an amazing job
There were four smaller tables
That would seat four each
And then the larger one in the middle
That table had eight seats
I was confused a bit
But I would see soon enough
It didn't matter either way
Because I was so in love
This room was simply breathtaking
My favorite colors tiffany blue and cream
Sebastian left no stone unturned
He had thought of everything

People started coming in
Saying how good it was to see me
Doing well and getting around
Being back on my feet
Then I saw my nurse
Ms. Ethel Wright
My mom admitted she cared for me like her own
Each and every night
She hugged me so tight
She was on vacation the day I was discharged

She gushed, "Look at you beautiful
We serve such a powerful God!"

Her energy consumed me
It was so light and sincere

"Thank you for coming
I'm so glad you're here."

She replied, "I was there at your worst
I surely wanted to see you at your best
And you look so beautiful tonight
In that gorgeous dress
You look amazing, Jaliyah
You are practically glowing
Happy from the inside out
You are so loved and it's showing."

"Thank you, Ms. Wright
That eighth seat must be for you
Join us at our family table
I now know that's what Sebastian wants to do."

The Cabin

Sebastian

<u>Everything in the world feels right,
seeing that smile on the face of my future wife.</u>

I entered the party room
And saw Jaliyah talking to her nurse
My heart was so full of love
I felt like I could burst
My dad was standing there
And he followed my gaze

He exhaled, "I wouldn't believe it if I hadn't seen it
My son in a love daze."

I took my parents over
It was time for them to meet the bride to be
She looked even more beautiful
When she turned towards me
She smiled, "Thank you baby
You did all of this for me!"

"Yes, my love and these two
Are surprise guests for the party
Meet my parents, your future in-laws
Colonel Patryk and Bethany Locklear."

Jaliyah shocked, revealed "Oh my gosh! I am so honored
I had no idea you two would be here
Thank you so much for coming."

My dad grinned, "Thanks for the invite."

My mom interjected, "Your energy is amazing, Jaliyah
Full of positivity and light."

Jaliyah

**<u>Greetings family and surprise guests.
I couldn't wait to see what came next.</u>**

I beamed, "Thank you, Mrs. Locklear
I see where Sebastian gets his eyes
You all are a beautiful family."
She replied softly, "Thank you Jaliyah and likewise."

"Patryk!" my dad yelled
As he and my mom walked in

"Malcolm!" Patryk declared

"It's been far too long my friend."

Sebastian and I walked back to the door
We still had guests to greet
We wanted to welcome everyone
Before taking our seats
I saw Jayson turn the corner
When he saw me, he smiled

I stated, "Jayson welcome back
For a much better reason this time."

Jayson

**<u>Open bar and a chill vibe.
I now see complete happiness in her eyes.</u>**

I saw Jaliyah and Sebastian
Standing at the door
She looked like herself again, beautiful
So much better than when I was here before

"Hello, Jaliyah
Thanks for inviting me."

She replied "Absolutely
It's a great night for a party."

Sebastian remarked, "Hi, Jayson
We'll be in in a sec
It's an open bar
So, help yourself."

"Thanks, Sebastian
I'll see you both inside
We'll be right behind you
We're nearing the end of the line."

I went inside
Spoke to Mr. and Mrs. Black
What an amazing room
I'm glad I came back
I grabbed a Hennessey and coke
And found my seat
I was happy to see nurse Wright
Seated next to me
The music choice was serene
I was enjoying the vibe
Everyone took their seats
It seems the last of the guests had arrived

LaRhonda N. Felton

Jaliyah

<u>Sebastian my lover, my friend. Soon to be my husband.</u>

Sebastian and I came in
And took our seats
His parents were next to him
And mine were seated beside me
Dinner tasted scrumptious
Everyone appeared to be having an amazing time
Dancing and laughing
I felt so grateful being alive
Sebastian stood up
Beckoned everyone to take their seats
And when I looked again
I saw him kneeling in front of me

"Jaliyah, I had no plans
Of falling in love with you
I didn't think it would ever happen for me
But look at what you made me do
You showed up in my life
A total surprise
Traveling alone at night
I was gone after one look in your eyes
Something shifted inside me
And I knew you were mine
It was like being struck by love
Like stopping time
I opened up
And told you all my secrets
I gave you my heart
Because I know you will keep it
You make me want to be better
To accomplish my dreams
I couldn't ask for a better queen
So, I'm asking again humbled and hopeful
Love me forever and share my life
Jaliyah Black, will you do me the honor of becoming my wife?

The Cabin

Jaliyah

<u>A breathtaking surprise and not one pair of dry eyes.</u>

My eyes were full of tears
And my makeup was a mess
But when Sebastian opened that box
I couldn't catch my breath
I'd never seen anything so beautiful
It was a Tiffany blue diamond ring
Emerald cut with baguettes
Now I was really crying
He placed the ring on my finger
And the whole room was on pause

He asked, "Baby your answer?"
I screamed, "Yes", to a raucous applause.

Almost everyone in the room
Had big smiles on their faces
Cheering us on and
Shouting congratulations
I happened to look at Jayson
And he merely tipped his glass
He looked indifferent
To be honest, he looked rather sad

Jayson

<u>I didn't expect to feel a finality so real.</u>

I sat there staring
Straight ahead
They were getting married
And inside I felt dead
Was I fooling myself?
Did I think I still had a chance?
Maybe deep down I was hoping they wouldn't last
But he proposed
And she said yes
She looked happy
Maybe this was best
And no matter how I tried
I couldn't force a smile
I came here for *this?*
Man, this was wild
I saw Jaliyah look my way
And I tipped my glass
I needed to find an exit
And get out of here fast

As I made my way to the exit
She caught me, "Jayson please don't leave, stay"
"Jaliyah, this is your celebration
And I don't want to be in the way."

She insisted, "You were invited
And I thought now we were friends
Or at least close to it
Call it a friendship on the mend."

"Jaliyah, don't get me wrong
I'm feeling things I didn't expect
I'm truly happy for you
Just not ready to see this yet

And you deserve it
To be in love, happy and whole
This just caught me off guard
Truth be told
Sebastian is a cool dude
Even I can see that
And you all seem so happy
Especially Mr. Black."

"That's because we are Jayson
I met Sebastian that day
My world ended as I knew it
The day I found out about you and Charae
I drove for hours
Alone in my car
I had no idea
I'd driven so far
I forgot all about
The renovations being done
I thought I would be by myself
And have the cabin alone
So, I do understand Jayson
If you're feeling a way
I understand if you leave
But I would love for you to stay."

I thought about it
And I put Jaliyah before me
I decided even though it hurt
This time I wouldn't leave

CHAPTER 20

LaRhonda N. Felton

Sebastian

<u>Sorry not sorry. I came to propose and party.</u>

I saw Jaliyah speaking with Jayson
Over by the door
I wasn't sure what happened
But Jaliyah was mine forevermore
I couldn't feel sorry for him
I was so happy for myself
He spectated in the game and lost
I played the hand I was dealt
I had been where he was
Fucked over a real one
But I wasn't losing out twice
I ain't never been that dumb
Jaliyah entered into my life
At the end of a long transition
She came at the perfect time
And I was in the right position
My mind is right
My game playing days are gone
She is the only woman I crave
She's the only woman I want to bone
I'm like the words to that hymn
I know I've been changed
And it's not too many men
That can say the same

The Cabin

Jaliyah

<u>The most beautiful night.</u>
<u>Weather brings memories that spark fright.</u>

We danced and we partied
Like it was nineteen ninety-nine
Needless to say
I had a damn good time
Everyone laughed
And we ate good food
I went to Sebastian's room
In an amazing mood
We made love until the sun came up
I woke up shaking and shivering
It was raining outside
And I tried to still my quivering
But I was a little too late
Sebastian pulled me close
I whispered, "Hold me tighter babe
And please don't ever let go."

The tears fell
Soaking his arms
He kissed my head
"Baby I got you, you're safe from harm
And as long as I'm around
I will protect you with my life
We will get through this
I promise you my future wife."

I must have dozed off
But when I woke up Sebastian was there
Still holding me tight
And kissing my hair
The rain had subsided
And I could finally breathe
I needed to work this out
I missed the old me

LaRhonda N. Felton

Jayson

<u>No reason to smile. I hadn't felt this low in a while.</u>

The party went on
Until late in the night
But I didn't wait around
I got on the road at first light
I left a note at the front desk
For Jaliyah and her fiancé
Thanking them for the invite
It was a wonderful soiree
I needed my own space
Their news was a trip
But it's what happens in life
And that can sometimes be a bitch
I would clear my head
Before my date tomorrow night
I wouldn't let my energy distract me
Besides Sasha could be Mrs. Right
Jaliyah was happy
And wanted us to be friends
I thought I wanted that too
But maybe I just wanted
To be in her life
And included in her plans
Not once did I picture
The presence of another man
I decided to back off
And keep my distance for a while
I knew I should be happy for her
But I still couldn't find a reason to smile

The Cabin

Jaliyah

<u>The unhealed traumas we face</u>
<u>will always invade our happy space.</u>

This past week
Moved slowly but felt short
I was apprehensive
About going to court
I would see Mike again
For the first time since that night
The coward beat me to a pulp
I nearly lost my life
In and out of consciousness
In a torturous spin
I was begging and pleading
Not knowing if it would ever end
The names he called me
While I lay writhing in pain
And all the while outside
It was a thunderous rain
He said I got him fired
And he had bills and a life too
And he was making sure
That Sebastian knew
He had fucked up
In a major way
Getting him fired
Over my clumsy mistake
But seeing him this time
At least I wouldn't be alone
And the prosecutor had promised
The sentencing wouldn't take long

LaRhonda N. Felton

Sebastian

<u>Sleepless nights until life feels right.</u>

Jaliyah didn't sleep
She tossed and turned all night
I'm glad the sentencing is today
So, we can catch this flight
I was going to look at a property
On the island of Bimini
And if all went well
I would be the new owner of a B&B
It was a six-bedroom seven-bathroom house
Three levels each with a master suite
A pool and Jacuzzi
With an ocean view that couldn't be beat
I knew Jaliyah needed a getaway
A complete and relaxing break
I could handle my business
And she could use the time escape
My parents were leaving
And so were the Blacks
Everyone should feel a little bit better
Once this ordeal is behind our backs

The Cabin

Jaliyah

<u>Face your terror or it possesses you forever.</u>

I wrote a victim's statement
But I decided I wouldn't share
I didn't need to subject my parents
To what truly went on there
They knew I was beaten
But they didn't know the depth of my fear
I was so deathly afraid
I would no longer be here
I wanted this part of my life
To be in my rearview mirror
I saw love and happiness in my future
And my vision was becoming increasingly clearer
I was still in therapy
And working through my pain
I was determined to get my life back
And end this suffering

We arrived at the courthouse
Sebastian on one side, my dad on the other
Sebastian's parents were close behind
Along with my mother
She tried to hide her fear
But I could see it in her face
But she was determined to protect me
With her fierceness and grace
We took our seats
Did the *all rise*
And I made direct contact
With those snake-like eyes
He smiled at me
But I couldn't pretend
Fear consumed me
Like I was in that cabin again

LaRhonda N. Felton

Sebastian put his arms around me
As I shivered in my seat
I couldn't continue to allow Mike
To have so much control over me
I needed to confront this
And I changed my mind
I was reading my statement
And prayed he received the maximum time

The judge told me to take my time
As I recalled the events
At first, I didn't look up
The energy in the room was too intense

"Michael Dodd first came to my family cabin
As part of the landscaping team
I didn't know him
And he didn't know me
He had left his toolbox
On the kitchen floor
And I ran into it
And nearly broke my toe
Unbeknownst to me
A complaint was filed
And Mike lost his job
That is what got him riled
The day he attacked me
I was at the cabin alone
He said his car had broken down
And asked to use the phone
I didn't think he was there
To hurt me or do me harm
I soon found out
In the worst way that I was wrong
He punched me so hard in my face
With a closed fist
I immediately fell to the floor
And almost lost consciousness

The Cabin

I begged and pleaded for him to stop
And it fell on deaf ears
He continued to beat me
And curse me through my blood and tears
I still suffer to this day
Especially when it rains
It's like I'm alone in that cabin
Enduring it all over again
So, I ask that the penalty is the maximum
And he loses that God-awful grin
No one should ever endure
My level of pain and suffering
He tried to kill me
He doesn't value life
He attacked me viciously
I didn't have a chance to fight
Thank you, Your Honor,
For allowing me to speak
I pray that he is required to pay
For what he's done to me."

I took my seat
And the judge didn't hesitate
To apply the maximum sentence
We all now knew his fate
Twenty-five years mandatory
With no time served
Thank God my prayers were answered
He got exactly what he deserved

Sebastian

<u>Don't dwell on the past because life comes at you fast.</u>

And just like that
Mike Dodd was a part of the past
I didn't feel sorry for him
Prison was safer for his ass
Jaliyah didn't flinch
Delivering her victim's speech
I got angry all over again
But I was proud of my baby
She held her own
And didn't fold one time
Jaliyah wasn't sure she could do it
Her resilience blew my mind
He left her for dead
And I'm thankful everyday
That my prayers were answered
And God allowed her to stay
I wished Bianca had let me in
She cheated us out of a friendship
I would always feel a twinge of guilt
For things turning out like this
I won't wallow in regret
Because the past can't be changed
I will continue to focus
On being a better man
Life is filled with uncertainties
I will persevere through the ebbs and flows
Face each day as a chance to be better
Than I was the day before

CHAPTER 21

LaRhonda N. Felton

Jaliyah

Finally a smile of peace because lately it's been eluding me.

The sigh of relief I breathed was audible
Heard throughout the courtroom
They had given me justice
And done what I needed them to do
We left the courthouse
Feeling lighter and more free
Resolved with the fact
That Mike would pay for what he did to me
My dad was headed to the realtor's office
To finalize the sale of the cabin
Even with everything going on
I couldn't believe *that* was happening
The cabin was his sanctuary
My dad had loved being there for years
And I didn't want his heart broken
Because of my fears

I called out to him, "Dad wait a minute
Please don't sell the cabin because of me
I know how much you love it
Maybe take some more time and don't be hasty."

"Jaliyah, this sale isn't just for you
It's for me and your mother too
How can we ever relax there again?
After what he put you through
Properties come and go
And they can always be replaced
But you my darling daughter
There is nothing that could ever take your place
Besides, I'm making a ridiculous profit
I keep telling you, Baby Girl
You and your mama are my life
My whole entire world."

I hugged my daddy
And kissed his left cheek

"I love you so much, Dad
Without you, there would be no me."

LaRhonda N. Felton

Jayson

Some shots you take and miss, but a real friend, calls you on your shit.

While my life was on an upswing
And I was enjoying going on dates
Part of me was very unhappy
And it made it hard to concentrate
I hadn't heard from Jaliyah
Since the night of her party
I almost wished I'd stayed a bit longer
And for that I was sorry
I thought of sending an email
Because I felt the need to explain
But I couldn't find a way
To apologize and hide my pain
When I put things together
I realized what happened
The night she didn't come home
Was the night she spent at the cabin
I guess then she met Sebastian
Or had she known him before
Their parents seemed close
I wanted to know more
Had she cheated on me?
And why did I still care?
I couldn't make sense of my feelings
And why I felt such despair
I called my boy Chris
Who had allowed me to sleep on his couch

"Let's meet up for a game of ball."

I needed to get out
My game was off
I was missing layups and free throws
He questioned, "What's up Jayson?
You're distracted and it shows."

The Cabin

We took a seat in the park
And I didn't know where to begin

I told him, "She's getting married."

He inquired, "By she, are we talking about Jaliyah again?"

"Yeah man
It's fucking with me too
I didn't think I would be this pressed."

He retorted, "Oh so you did love her, *who knew*?"

"What the fuck does that mean?"
I questioned and I was mad

Chris retorted, "Don't get out of pocket bro
I feel sorry for your ass
We all get that *one* woman
That is down to ride
And you had that with Jaliyah
But you had too much pride."

"*Pride?* Man come on."

"Tell me what it was then
That kept you from telling her about losing your job
And start secretly fucking her best friend?
Pride dumb ass!
Look I understand
I know that hurt
But it's not the end man
What about the new shorty?
You said she was fine."

"She is man, but she's not Jaliyah
This marriage shit is blowing my mind."

"And why is that dude?
You had to know she would find someone else
Jaliyah's don't come around every day
Fine, sexy, smart and can take care of herself
Dude look, you fucked up
But it's not the end of the world
You need to either fight for her
Or make it work with old girl."

"Jaliyah deserves to be happy
I don't want to ruin that."

"Then suck that shit up
And take off that ugly ass hat."

I laughed, "Damn dawg
Your advice is fantastic."

He chuckled, "I know, now get your ass on this court
And focus on making baskets."

Sebastian

A picturesque escape, washes the troubles away.

We said our goodbyes at the airport
And boarded our separate flights
I was so excited to be sleeping
Under the Bimini sky tonight
Jaliyah seemed relaxed
We flew first class
I wasn't about to be cramped in coach
Or boarding last
Jaliyah deserved the best
And I was making sure she had it
Besides, she had grown up with nothing less
First class was a habit
I needed to show her father
That I was a man like him
And taking care of her was first and foremost
In my head it was a small competition
Not to be just as good
But slightly better than
After all, he was her dad
But I was her man
The flight was smooth
Before long we prepared to land
I could see the turquoise waters
And stretches of white sand
Jaliyah whispered "Oh my gosh
This place looks amazing"
I agreed, "It sure does
Let's have some fun my baby."

LaRhonda N. Felton

Jaliyah

Dreams do come true, don't hesitate, move!

We made it to the property
And Sebastian had picked a winner
This place was breathtaking
The current owner was making us dinner
Each master suite
Had an ocean view
Windows from floor to ceiling
And the showers had marble tile too

I screeched, "Sebastian this place has to be a fortune."

He remarked, "It's well worth the asking price
Our guests will cover the overhead
And there's an office where you can write
I will fish and shop
And prepare the meals
I can make any needed repairs."

"Baby, this can't be real."

He pinched my butt
I yelled, "Ouch!
He kissed my lips
I asked, "What was that about?"
"To show you it's real
And this isn't a dream
This can be our life
It's so peaceful and serene."

"Sebastian, I trust you
So, lets seal the deal
I want to get married here
This place is perfect, I am loving the feel

The Cabin

The energy is clean
I love the uninterrupted flow
Let's make this place ours
Hurry up now, go"

LaRhonda N. Felton

Sebastian

**<u>Dreams come to sleepers, but they become your reality
when you're riding with a keeper.</u>**

I laughed and confessed
"That is what I wanted to hear
I was praying you would love it."

As I smiled from ear to ear
I talked to the owner
And let him know our decision
He and his wife were ecstatic
Jaliyah was excited and could see my vision

We opened a bottle of champagne
And celebrated with a toast
Another two bottles of wine with dinner
All involved were doing the most

Jaliyah and I talked half the night
Making plans on redecorating
She planned to spare no expense
I would do anything for my baby
She shared my dream with me
And was willing to make it come true
I realized in that exact moment
That's what people in love do

Jaliyah

<u>Iridescent scene. Peaceful and serene.</u>

I woke up before the sun
Which was part of my plan
Sebastian was still sleeping
He was such a gorgeous man
I went out to the beach
To watch the sun rise
And say my morning prayer
I couldn't believe my eyes
The colors were amazing
Oranges, yellows, and reds
I was abundantly blessed
And I needed this time to clear my head
I felt somewhat relieved
Like I was on the other side of a bad dream
But I couldn't let my guard down
Because this was my life, my reality
And while all of this is true
I wasn't going to wallow in the grief
Or even self-pity
I am taking the steps to find relief
To be whole again
Not just flashes in the pan
But to maintain some rhythm
Returning to the woman that I know I am
Jayson crossed my mind
He left without a proper goodbye
Maybe he just couldn't see me being happy
Especially with another guy
Either way I'm not to blame
He realized what he had a little too late
I asked for space
But I never said I planned to wait
Finding love so suddenly after our breakup
Surprised me too

Falling for Sebastian
Was the last thing I planned to do

But it happened
It's how my life unfolds
And I'm thankful and happy
Truth be told
I have no malice for Jayson
I truly wish him the best
And maybe we could've worked it out
Had he been a man and confessed
But he didn't
And now it's water under the bridge
I wasn't going to hang around
To see if it happened again
Enough of my stroll down memory lane
As I dug my toes deeper into the white sand
I realized I had work to do
I had my wedding to plan

Jayson

<u>Uninvited guests moving too fast.</u>
<u>It seems I made a mistake with Sasha's ass.</u>

When you're grinding
Time does fly
I didn't even realize
That the last two months flew by
Charae was due to deliver
Any day now
And I had to dump this new chick
Very soon somehow
She was clingy
And a nuisance
Getting her to understand boundaries
Was proving redundant and useless
Sasha was moving way too fast
To be in a relationship
I told her I just wanted to date
But she didn't give a shit
She was popping up to my spot
All different times of night
I left her ass knocking
Turned off all my lights
I go to leave for work the next morning
Shorty sitting on my truck
She said her girlfriends had dropped her off
I'm thinking that's fucked up

I told her, "It's not cool
To just stop by."

She laughed, "Well you are my boyfriend."

I reminded her, "That's a lie
You and I aren't exclusive
We date from time to time

Excuse me I need to get to work
Do you need me to call you a ride?"

She told me no, her cousin was coming
Since she'd been outside all night
And that the way I treated her wasn't right
I told her I didn't know she was outside
And I would talk to her when I got off
But I hadn't followed through
With one single call
She was blowing my phone up
So, her ass had to go
I wasn't compromising
The answer was a point-blank no
I checked my mailbox
Before I headed inside
And with the envelope I saw
I nearly died
That Tiffany blue color she loves
A wedding invitation
On the island of Bimini
Did I even want this vacation?

Sebastian

**<u>So much to do, so little time.
I'm determined to please this fiancée of mine.</u>**

As I marked items off
My honey-do list
I remembered there was
One thing I missed
I called Maverick
My best man
I let him know
What I needed for my plan
It was for Jaliyah
A wedding surprise
I couldn't wait to see
The excitement in her eyes
Maverick couldn't believe
I was doing it again
Taking the plunge
And becoming a husband
We ran through a lot of chicks
Back in my playa days
And Maverick was still running
Even with a wife and baby
I didn't judge him
Hell, we used to be one in the same
But I needed something different
Which is why I gave up the game
But I couldn't wait to see him
To hang and catch up
He was flying in early
And Jaliyah was making a fuss
She had completely redecorated
And I admit it looked nice
I told her with all the new amenities
We would need to raise the price

Our first paying guests
Wouldn't arrive until after our honeymoon
But that was the least of our worries
Both sets of parents would be here soon
They were each staying in one
Of the master suites
Maverick and a few more relatives
Were also staying in our retreat
The house would be full
Since the first time we moved in
But it wouldn't be strangers this time
All family and friends
Jaliyah insisted on the third floor being ours
It had a panic room with a private escape
I would've added whatever she needed
To make her feel safe
She had become more comfortable
More confident as time passes
She was less jumpy now when it rained
Thanks to therapy and self-defense classes

The Cabin

Jaliyah

<u>**Preparations underway for our beautiful wedding day.**</u>

Invitations mailed, ordered my cake
My dress was on its final alteration
And our parents were on the way
I was having an elegant ceremony
But nothing too large
I didn't hire a coordinator
So, I was in charge
Sebastian and I split the list
He had food and drinks
The photographer was local
That was all for today, I think
I was having a small shower
With family and a few friends
And Sebastian was going out for drinks
To hang out with the men
Everything was flowing smoothly
The mail came with an RSVP
It was from Jayson
I was glad he was coming
It means he had put aside
His pride and decided to celebrate
He didn't list a plus one
So, he wasn't bringing a date
I thought twice about
Sending Jayson the invite
But he had been kind enough to come
And see about me after that awful night
He didn't seem very happy at the party
And he left for home the very next day
But I took the chance
And sent the invitation anyway
In just a few days
I would be a married lady
Living on an island
With my husband, my baby

CHAPTER 22

LaRhonda N. Felton

Sebastian

<u>Old dog, same tricks.</u>
<u>I turned in my player card, I was done with it.</u>

I was at the airport waiting
The last few days wore me out
I hadn't gotten much sleep
Being out and about
I was getting impatient
Maverick's flight was late
Everyone was waiting for me
We had reservations at eight
I called my dad and told him to gather the guys
And head over to the spot
I didn't want Jaliyah's shower affected
His plane landing is the best news I got
I saw my boy come through the doors

"It's about damn time!"

Maverick commented, "Man, who are you telling?
I almost lost my mind."

We dapped each other up
And did our brotherly hug
He confessed, "Man I can't believe it
Your ass bit by the love bug
She must be special
To make you propose
But you have grown up."

"A little, I suppose
After my messy ass divorce
Man, please, I turned in my card
You should try it, Mav
It's not that hard."

The Cabin

"You crack me up Bash
And that is bullshit
I'm on the prowl tonight
Looking for a thot to hit."

"Hey, I'm the last one to judge
But do you *ever* think about your wife?"

"Yes, I think about her
But I ain't thinking about her tonight
Bash, you know my shit was different
She trapped me with a baby
I wouldn't have ever gotten married
I never wanted to be tied to one lady
Man, we roamed the streets
And shared a lot of fun times
And she comes up pregnant
Ruining the life I had in mind
And I know ruin is a strong word
But sometimes that's how it feels
And I can't change it
But that's the real
I'm getting a vasectomy
She got one but no more
And I have fourteen years left
My daughter just turned four
Besides, I think she does her own thing
Or at least she should
Because I very rarely touch her
Even though I could."

"Damn dawg, I didn't know
It was that bad
Why even stay together?
She must be miserable and sad."

"No, to be honest
She loves being my wife

Which is fucked up to me
I don't even try to do right."

"But what kind of example
Are you setting for your child?"

"Damn that's a point I hadn't
Considered in a while."

We rode the rest of the way
Catching up talking shit
Maverick was silent on the hard issues
But I was used to it

The Cabin

Jaliyah

<u>Congratulations! Drinks and conversations.</u>

The ladies and I waited around
For the men to finally leave
I didn't know what would happen
Or what they had up their sleeves
I had a few friends from college
That were gracious enough to make the trip
My cousins and my mom had planned the shower
Down to the chips and dip
We went out on the seaside deck
And they poured me an amazing drink
Something with pineapple and rum
The liquid was blue and the umbrella pink
We had a great girls' night
Laughing at our men
I was surrounded by over a hundred years of marriage
And I got some jaw-dropping advice in the end
After everyone had separated
Sebastian's mom pulled me aside

She confided, "I was hesitant at first
I won't even lie
I didn't think he was ready
To walk down the aisle again
Or that he'd matured enough
To be anyone's husband
But I was wrong
Being here has shown me
He has done a lot of work on himself
And he's still working
Sometimes it takes the right person
To come along at the right time
And I'm so grateful God sent you
To that son of mine
Don't be timid with him
Or afraid to speak up

That was Bianca's downfall
God bless, he ran all over her."

She hugged me so tight
And her energy was so sincere
"Welcome to our family Jaliyah
Call me if you ever need me and I'll be here."

I pulled back and questioned
"What if I just want you around?"
She laughed, "You just say the word
I will be island bound."

The Cabin

Sebastian

**<u>Cigars, Cognac and VIP.
The men I love here to celebrate with me.</u>**

We arrived at the club
And headed for the VIP
Everyone was in back
Waiting for me
Maverick stopped at the bar

He asked, "What? I'm ordering a drink."

"Man, we have waiters in VIP."

"You're right Bash, I didn't think."

Malcolm and my dad were chopping it up
Smoking a couple of cigars

My dad sighed, "Finally you're here
We're putting in an order at the bar."

I greeted the other few guys
And got ready to party
They had waited long enough for me
For us to get started
Maverick was quiet
Which for him was odd
But tonight, was about me
And I planned to party hard

LaRhonda N. Felton

Jayson

<u>Confused feelings and drinks will never help when you need to think.</u>

I didn't make the bachelor party
Since I had to catch the redeye
I checked into my room
And I begin to ponder why
Why had I come?
Was it really to celebrate?
This marriage didn't make *me* happy
It still wasn't too late
I could go back to the airport
And simply leave
No harm done
No one had even seen me
But on the same hand
I don't want to leave this place
I need to see if she does it
If she can marry another man in my face
I felt anxious
And I know I shouldn't be
Because if I'd never cheated
Jaliyah would still be with me
I thought damn, damn, damn Jayson
You really fucked up
And you spent all this money
To watch them pledge their love
I got a drink
From the bar in the room
I sat on the bed
And felt the emptiness loom
I decided to drink
Until at some point I passed out
Inebriation was the only way I could silence
The anger I wanted to spout

Jaliyah

<ins>The woman that gave me life, on the day I become a wife.</ins>

I woke the next morning
To a beautiful sunrise
It was my wedding day
As the tears filled my eyes
There was a knock on my door
And my mom requested to come in

I answered, "Sure Mom"
Let this day begin

"Jaliyah, I have something for you
It's your something old, your dad has your new
Your *mother in love* has your borrowed
And well, that ring is your blue."

My mom cajoled, "Sit with me
This comb is a family heirloom
It's been passed down for generations
And you will keep it to pass on to your daughter soon."

"Mom, don't rush me
I want to enjoy being a wife."

My mom chuckled, "Oh you will
Almost every night."

I laughed at the idea
As she helped me get dressed
She cried, "You're so beautiful Sunshine
But I didn't expect anything less."

LaRhonda N. Felton

Sebastian

<u>A familiar face at the wrong time, in the wrong place.</u>

I must admit
I'm a little nervous
Everyone was taking their seats
Preparing for our service
I was standing at the altar
When I saw Jayson take his seat
He looked hung-over
And he was glaring at me
I hoped he hadn't come
To simply show his ass
Because just like Mike
He was not getting a pass

Maverick was behind me
And he leaned in and whispered
"Who is he?
Why does he look familiar?"

"He's Jayson, Jaliyah's ex
The one that cheated with her friend."

"Oh okay
And why is he here again?"

"He was cool for a while
I mean we might've been friends
But maybe I read him wrong
And his true intention is to cause ruin."

I heard Maverick whisper, "Oh shit!"

But I couldn't ask what
Because The Wedding March began to play
And the guests stood up

The Cabin

Jaliyah

<u>As much as things change, some behaviors remain the same.</u>

My dad held me tightly
As I nervously walked down the aisle
I was shaking so bad
I almost forgot to smile
But when I saw Sebastian
And the look on his face
The butterflies left my stomach
And love filled their place
I never knew I could feel this happy
And I wanted time to stand still on this day
So, I could always and forever
Feel this way
I saw Jayson sitting there
Like he wanted to leap from the seat
He had anger written all over him
But he wasn't looking at me
I followed his gaze
But I didn't know what had happened
Was he staring at Maverick?
Or could it be Sebastian?

I got to the altar
And Sebastian took my hand
God knows he was fine
And in a few minutes, he'd be my husband
I saw Jayson get up
Out of the corner of my eye
God what is he doing?
And more importantly *why*?
He was coming my way
But my dad blocked his path
I could hear a few people in the audience
Make an audible gasp

Jayson wasn't budging
And that caused Sebastian's dad to intervene
Why did Jayson come here?
To make a damn scene
The officiant kept going
As Jayson was escorted inside
Sebastian couldn't hide his anger
And to be honest neither could I
A beautiful day, my day
Filled with family and friends
And the thing people will remember most is
Jayson and his damn shenanigans

The Cabin

Jayson

<u>I knew I should've gone home.</u>
<u>This way, I would've never known.</u>

As I got inside, Malcolm let me go
But I had an attitude
I yelled, "What the hell, Malcolm?
And who is this old dude?"

Malcolm retorted, "Watch your damn mouth
Jayson what's the big idea?
If you couldn't handle it
You shouldn't have come here."

Jayson confessed, "I didn't think she would do it
But that's beside the point
You want her to get hurt?
Is that what you want?"

"What in the hell are you talking about?
Sebastian loves Jaliyah
Now I'm asking you again
Why did you even come here?
She thought you two could be friends
But you came here to bring her more pain
Didn't you do enough of that
Sleeping with her best friend?"

"I'm not the only one…"

"What are you trying to say?"

"Ask Sebastian's best man
How well he knows Charae
I'm surprised you don't know
You seem to know everything else
Oh, but let me keep quiet
I am here by myself."

Malcolm replied, "Wait a damn minute
We need to get something straight
You interrupted my daughter's wedding
Over Maverick and Charae?"

"Well they're best friends aren't they
Usually one in the same
Sebastian will hurt Jaliyah
Playing the same game."

"Son look, I feel bad for you
But your reasoning makes no sense
Jaliyah is nothing like Charae
So, you must see there can be a difference."

"I saw that dude with Charae
When she was blaming her baby on me
Turns out her child isn't mine
But Maverick out there *is* the daddy."

"Listen Jayson, you're grasping at straws
This news affects Jaliyah *how?*
I'm in here arguing with your ass
Missing my daughter take her vows
I should go upside your head
But let me get back
You can let yourself out."

"Thanks for nothing Mr. Black."
I left through the front
And I was enraged
I shouldn't have come here
This wasn't something I was ready to face
Damn! This wasn't supposed to happen
I promised myself I would remain cool
But leave it to me
To act a damn fool

The Cabin

I made it back to the hotel
And packed my suitcase
I would pay whatever it cost
To get the hell out of this place

CHAPTER 23

Jaliyah

<u>No way Satan, not today! We are getting married anyway.</u>

I saw my dad come back outside
Right at the exchange of our vows
I'm sure like me everyone was wondering
What that commotion was all about
I heard the officiant say
You are now pronounced husband and wife
You may kiss your bride
I felt robbed of the most important day of my life
Sebastian and I kissed
While the guests applauded
But I needed to know about the disruption
And what the hell had caused it

The Cabin

Sebastian

<u>**Shit hit the fan. Thanks a lot best man.**</u>

"What the fuck was that?"
I was beyond livid

"Where the fuck is Jayson?
I am going to kill him."

My dad grabbed me
And pulled me to the side

"Son, watch your temper."

But his anger he couldn't hide

"The one day! One fucking day!
The most beautiful day of our lives
Ruined by jealousy and envy..."
I watched the tears fall from my wife's eyes

Malcolm came up
"Let's take this inside."
He turned to our guests smiling
"The bar is open you all have a good time."
Thankfully, everyone went towards the bar
The seven of us went into the kitchen
Malcolm requested, "You two take a seat
And I need you both to listen.
Jaliyah, Jayson wasn't ready
To watch you marry someone else
He thought he could handle it
But he embarrassed us, as well as himself.
His behavior was deplorable
Asinine and senseless
But he thought he was saving Jaliyah
He just couldn't witness this

However, Maverick your name came up
Let's get things straight
Jayson told us
That he caught you with Charae."

Now I'm truly shocked
And this was all too much
I looked from my dad to Malcolm
And questioned, "Mav, what the fuck?
Man come on
Tell me it's not true
How in hell do you know *her?*"

Maverick looked confused
"Bash come on now
I didn't know Charae was the friend
I hadn't put two and two together
Until I saw Jayson come in
I met Charae a while back
Like two years ago
And we would hook up from time to time
Nothing serious, you know
But shorty crazy
Blaming her baby on me."

My dad interjected
"Well Jayson reported *you* are the daddy."
Malcolm chimed in too
"That's what he said
He told us, it's not him
So, it must be you instead."

I watched my best man
As the blood drained from his face
"Man, Mav your shit is catching
Up with you all over the place."

"I'm sorry, Bash, I didn't know
That's what made bro act a fool

He recognized me
But he was on some other shit too."

Maverick had a point
I mean what would've been accomplished
If Jayson confronted Maverick
Whatever they had going on, wasn't going to stop this

I took Jaliyah's hand and tugged her,
"Let's go wife
Our day had a hiccup
But it will still be one hell of a night."

LaRhonda N. Felton

Jaliyah

<u>Love wins, even with a crazy spin.</u>

I took Sebastian's hand
And we headed back outside
We had people to entertain
Before we said our goodbyes
Our honeymoon was full of islands
A beach hopper's dream
And every beach we touched
We would be christening
Although I wasn't surprised
About Charae and Maverick
I hoped she was breaking herself
Out of those bad habits
With a baby on the way
She needed to be a better example
Or that kid would be just like her
A whole damn handful

The Cabin

Jayson

<u>Plane after plane. Nearly drove me insane.</u>

It was late but
I was home
It was layover after layover
All the way home
I couldn't believe it
I fucked up
And a million apologies
Would never be enough
I'm not over Jaliyah yet
And I may never shake her
My phone buzzed with a text
It read *"Charae is in labor"*
Too damn bad
She would deliver alone
Maybe her mom is there
Cause her baby daddy ain't home
I took my shower
And poured me a drink
I was so fucking exhausted
I didn't even want to think

LaRhonda N. Felton

Jaliyah

<u>Exquisite wedding night, runs into early morning flight.</u>

It was after two
Before we finally laid down
And we had to be up at six
To prepare to leave town
But I was excited
Ready to leave
With my sexy loving husband
Right next to me
And as if on cue
He pulled me close with his lips on my back
I turned over
And straddled his lap
We made love for the first time
As husband and wife
I had multiple hard orgasms
For the rest of the night
We donned sunglasses
Even in the early morn
Because both of us looked
Like we'd been filming porn

The Cabin

Sebastian

<u>Completely in love and joining the mile-high club.</u>

I looked over at my wife
Sitting in first class
And all I wanted was
Our love to last
She was so beautiful
And all mine
Round ass and hips
Damn she fine

I put my hand on her thigh
She licked her lips seductively
I whispered in her ear while sucking her lobe
"In a few minutes, come find me."
I went into the lavatory
Waiting on my love
She came in
And we joined the mile-high club
I put her on the counter
Flipped the door sign to occupied
Got on my knees
And put my face between her thighs
She stifled her moans
By biting her lips
I kept hitting her spot
She kept shouting, "Shit!"
And right after she came
I slid deep inside
She was squeezing me tight
And blowing my mind
My wife was my sexual match
My freak in the sheets
She stumbled into my life
An angry beautiful mystery
I planned day in and day out
To keep her happy and satisfied

LaRhonda N. Felton

Thanks for fucking up Jayson
Because Jaliyah Black-Locklear is mine

Epilogue

Jayson

Growth and change. Just a year ago, I wasn't the same.

It's been almost a year
Since Jaliyah and I last spoke
And I figured she must be happy
Or at the very least I hoped
My job had promoted me
And I was moving to DC
It was all for the best
I would be closer to my family
Charae had her baby
And she and the nosey neighbor got engaged
She admitted Maverick had shown up to her house
Acting a fool and enraged
His wife had finally left him
Packed up all her shit
While he was in Bimini
Somehow she'd gotten an anonymous tip
That his ass had fucked up
And had a baby on the way
Obviously, she'd finally had enough
Of his ass that day
Charae said he had been drinking
And he looked bad
But she didn't let him near the baby
She called the cops on his ass
I listened as she talked
And chuckled to myself
I didn't have any kids
But I know how he felt
To be on the losing end
While your world falls apart
And you have no one to blame
Because you were at fault from the start

LaRhonda N. Felton

I think of Jaliyah
From time to time
If I said I didn't wish things were different
I'd be lying
But it was over for us
And I was moving on
As for this city and the memories
I was saying so long
Maybe one day
I would see her again
And maybe just maybe
We could finally be friends

The Cabin

Jaliyah

<u>One year down, a lifetime to go.</u>
<u>I would say yes a million times more.</u>

"Baby, wake up!
And eat cake with me
Wake up my sexy man
It's our anniversary!"

Sebastian turned over
Groggily replying, "Yes it sure is
I love you baby
Happy anniversary, Mrs. Locklear."

We had cake and champagne for breakfast
And then we made love on the deck
It had been a whole year
And I was looking forward to the next
I wanted an entire lifetime
With Sebastian by my side
Turning dreams into reality
With this beautiful man of mine
I belong to him
And he belongs to me
As we watch the turquoise waters
Roll over our feet

I found him on a day
When I felt my world had shattered
But he was my destiny
My protector when it mattered
Sebastian the man of my dreams
A dream I had yet to imagine
And it all happened the night
I drove to the cabin

The End

Acknowledgments

Always first and foremost, I give all thanks and praise to my Lord and Savior, Jesus Christ. Without Him, I wouldn't be here. I would not be able to share this magnificent gift that He's bestowed upon me.

I had no plans to publish anything this year. Evidently, God had other plans for me.

To my mom, Phyllis Felton, and my sister, Melissa Felton-Henderson, I give the ultimate thanks. I love you both. Your enthusiasm and excitement as this poetic love story took on a life of its own propelled me to keep writing. Jaliyah and Sebastian came to life due to the insatiable appetite you two shared for their love.

To my brother, Lindsey 'Scooter' Felton, I love you to life. Thank you. Your unwavering love and support propels me to strive for greater. You never forget to reiterate how proud I've made you by sharing my passion with the world.

My brother in love, Derrick Henderson, and my sister in love, Alfred 'Freda' Clark, I love you bot. Your support means the world to me. Our family is blessed to have you both in it.

To my nieces and nephews: Whew! I have a special bond with each of you in some way. I pray that I have inspired you all. Always reach for the galaxies beyond the stars. Be limitless while turning your dreams into reality.

My Meeting of The Minds Book Club sisters: You ladies are my beta readers, my sounding board and an amazing support system. Thank you, ladies, from the bottom of my heart… Toni Cash, Joye Powell and Janaver Wooden. I love you all!

Special thanks to my bonus sister, Monica 'Monet' Coleman. Sis, you encouraged me, prayed for and with me. The countless hours of conversation and support mean so much more than you can ever imagine. I love you, Sis.

Thank you, Detrice 'Dee-Dee' Jackson. Your excitement and encouragement are so appreciated. Your willingness to promote and strategize with me is priceless. I love you!

My editor and publisher, Liltcra R. Williams: I appreciate you more than you know. I thank you for pushing me to dig a little deeper each time; ensuring that my words and creativity are conveyed in a way that drives the point home, but never wavering from being my own.

Special thanks to Ms. JoAnne McGriff-Hillord, Torrance 'T-Man' Smith, Latisha Nicole Felton, Kwatishea Dorsey, Bennie Cummings and Etrec J. White.

Thank you for your support, Ethelene Walker, Gloria Jamise Barnett, Janice Parker, Toshid Jones and Megan Newell Cason. Thanks to Aaron Woodson and The Author's Roundtable.

To my readers, I thank you so very much. Thank you for supporting and embracing my love for bringing words to life. Thank you for the reviews and feedback you have provided. I hope *The Cabin* brings you as much joy and excitement reading it as it did for me writing it.

Keep on reading! There's more to come.

~The Poetic Gemini

LaRhonda N. Felton

About the Author

Author LaRhonda N. Felton is a Florida native. Her love for writing was recognized and nurtured early. After winning second place in a short story contest in 8th grade, she then went on to have one of her poems published in a national anthology. However, it took more time to fully acknowledge her undying passion for the craft.

With a myriad of life experiences to draw from, LaRhonda's forward-thinking ideas on love and life soon began to pour out at an uncontrollable rate. LaRhonda decided to loosen her self-censorship and learned how to simply let the words flow, no longer concerned about who the truth may offend. This unrestricted freedom of expression allowed her to discover a personal niche, strictly focusing on love and the erotic aspects of adulthood.

In The Meantime is her first published collection of poetry; *The Dual Sides of My Gemini Mind* is her second; and her third release is *The Cabin*. LaRhonda has composed a vast selection of poems with four more extended rhyme scheme stories on standby.